Marketing and promotion will include a national media campaign, bookseller/librarian outreach, digital advertising, targeted newsletters, social posts, and giveaways.

For more information, contact:
Rachel Fershleiser, Associate Publisher,
Executive Director of Marketing
rachel.fershleiser@catapult.co

Things We
Found When
the Water
Went Down

Things We Found When the Water Went Down

· A NOVEL ·

Tegan Nia Swanson

CATAPULT  NEW YORK

Copyright © 2022 by Tegan Nia Swanson

ISBN: 978-1-64622-169-1

Library of Congress Control Number: TK

Cover design by Dana Li
Book design by Laura Berry

Catapult
New York, NY
books.catapult.co

Printed in the United States of America

1 3 5 7 9 10 8 6 4 2

To Margaret Pennington Swanson
teller of stories, advocate, water-hearted matriarch,
the One Who First Shared the Magic of the Inland Sea with me

What would happen if one woman told the truth about her life?
The world would split open

—MURIEL RUKEYSER, from "Käthe Kollwitz" in
The Speed of Darkness

Contents

Things We
Found When
the Water
Went Down

29 November 2016

They found Hugo Mitchum facedown in the water and the lily-weeds, thanks to the bloody trail someone left behind when they dragged him through the snow.

It was a warm winter but Ruin had frozen over partially, so it was difficult to pull his body out. Men on the volunteer fire crew kept falling through the ice, sinking into that frigid, dirty water, up to their shins, their knees, their hips.

Maybe we should just leave him here till summer, someone suggested. *He'd've done the same, ya know.*

Deputy Ranger Ingrid Solberg-Black of the Caelais Co. Wilderness Service came with a winch and her sled dogs. She would tell me later *he looked like a sacka moldy potatoes. Except those buckshot holes in his throat.*[1] It was her and her dogs who finally yanked Hugo Mitchum free.

Two days later, my mother would be taken into custody. Dad was at work in the North Country, but the two of us were at the cabin on Little Ghost Loon alone. Heard the police were on their way by word over shortwave.

She knew it was coming. Fuck, the whole town knew it was coming. They looked away.[2]

· · · · · · · · · · · · · · · · · ·

1. Чеховское ружьё. See also: pp. TK.
2. I would later realize she'd known for years. My mother was never a gentle presence. Certainly rubbed some the wrong way. But it was after the Fight at the Windigo the summer of 1999 that two young Mesabi mining men, Ellis Olsen, seventeen, of the North Country, and Hugo Mitchum, twenty-one, of Beau Caelais, might have had particular reason to be upset with sixteen-year-old Marietta. See also: p. TK.

COMMON LOON[3]

(*Gavia*[4] *immer*)

known colloquially as   *hell-diver*

&   *call-up-a-storm*

from the Swedish *emmer*[5]

see also:

immergo[6]
& *immersus*[7]

lúinn[8]
lam[9]

for its eerie cry[10]

the Old Norse *lómr*   meaning *lament*.

. . . .

3. In reference to the bird's discomfort on dry land; in comparison, at least, to its grace and elegance in the water.
4. Genus *Gavia*, meaning *unidentified seabird*.
5. The gray or blackened ashes of a fire [referring to its dark plumage].
6. Latin, *to immerse*.
7. *Submerged*.
8. Icelandic, *worn-out* or *fatigued*.
9. Swedish, *lame*.
10. What Thoreau once described as *the wildest sound ever heard here*.

Dramatis Personae

EMALENE BEATRICE (ABERNATHY) BAILEY: me, Lena. She/her(s). Daughter of Marietta, Patrick. Archivist. The One Who Came of the Solstice.

MARIETTA ABERNATHY[11]: my mother. She/her(s). Daughter of Ursa, the Hunter. Curator of the Paper Moon Menagerie. The One Who Drowned and Came Back.

PATRICK BAILEY: Dad. He/him/his. Son of unknown woman, J. A. Bailey. Hydraulic specialist, Ironsen & Associates. Singer of hymns, player of resonators. The One Who Carries Us to Shore Like a Wave.

BEATRICE ORLEANS: Aunt Bea. She/they/her(s)/them/theirs. Child of Marie, Joseph. Lover of Ursa, adoptive parent of Marietta. Social worker, Sunday House for Girls of Caelais County. Current owner-operator, the Bear & Bird. The One Who Laughs and Laughs.

URSA ABERNATHY: Matriarch. She/her(s). Daughter of Dot, Henry. The Mountain Who Bled Out in the Snow.

ELLIS OLSEN: the Ghost of Beau Caelais. He/him/his. Son of Elin, Ole. Mining apprentice, Mesabi Mine Co., Ruin Lake Branch. The Witness.

HUGO MITCHUM: the Weasel of the North Country. He/him/his. Son of Rita Mae, Arthur. Mining apprentice, Mesabi Mine Co., Ruin Lake Branch. The One Who Digs the Hole.

FRANCIS DELACROIX II: Frank, to those who know. He/him/his.

. . . .

11. My mother had many names. For a complete list, see p. TK.

Son of Roberta, Francis. Officer, Caelais County Aquatic Patrol; retired site chief, Mesabi Mine Co., Ruin Lake Branch. The Law Uneasy.

INGRID SOLBERG-BLACK: Deputy ranger and de facto advocate. She/her(s). Daughter of Lisle, Walter. Posted at the Ruin Lake Station, Caelais Co. Wilderness Service, c. 1998–present. The Soft Hand That Carries an Axe.

THE DOGS: the silver Wolf-Sister, the Shepherd Who Watches, and the Spotted One who curls up at my feet whenever we are still.

and **THE WOMEN   BENEATH**

Now

Please find herein: the following results of my personal investigation into the events of 20 June 1999 and all that came thereafter, conducted during the Snowstorm into Which My Mother Vanished, in and around Beau Caelais and the North Country, c. Dec. 2016.

Primary documents and secondary source materials include but are not limited to: found objects, excerpts of journals, letters, interviews, and public records [e.g., documentation by law enforcement, court transcripts, newspaper articles, land treaties, and leases].

Some content has been included in its original form; others have been referenced, or replicated here, as faithfully as is possible for preservation's sake.

Also included are editorial recollections and imagined estimations based upon available facts and observations.

Information will appear in nonlinear fashion, unless otherwise noted by time stamp, you may assume material presented is voiced from a point of view anchored in the Time of the Production of This Artifact,

> meaning:
> I am sharing it with you in as close to *now* as is possible,
> given we are not also sharing a brain or a body.

Where appropriate, editorial annotation by footnote is provided for context and pertinent tangential content.

If you get lost, please refer to the Map.

BEAU CAELAIS & THE INLAND SEA[12]

[excerpt, letter from my mother]

1 DEC.

My dear, if you are ever lost on the mainland, orient yourself like a compass and look North.

On clear days, you'll see our house on Little Ghost Loon—or at least the roof and the star-loft—but in fog or stormy water, our island will be swallowed by the Inland Sea, the North Country losing its ice. To the East lie miles of dead stumps, moose racks, unending ash from the Fire. Aunt Bea has photographs of old-growth black pine and whistling birch tacked to the wall at the bar, but the paper is beginning to yellow and fade and it's best not to get caught up in things already missing. To the South is Ruin Lake; downhill the remains of Ellis Olsen's hut. What is left of the water shines iridescent in weak sun. Use it like a mirror. Use it as a reminder. It is hard to reconcile what is with what used to be. It is hard, too, to ignore the smell of whatever spunk Hugo Mitchum spilled in the slurry.

Straight West is Beau Caelais. I'm not certain what you might find beyond.

....

12. See Map, p. TK. The Inland Sea, the Boundary Islands, and Beau Caelais, the latter meaning *beautiful* and *in color, an indescribable blue comparable only to the deepest, shifting hues of sky reflected upon calm waters.*

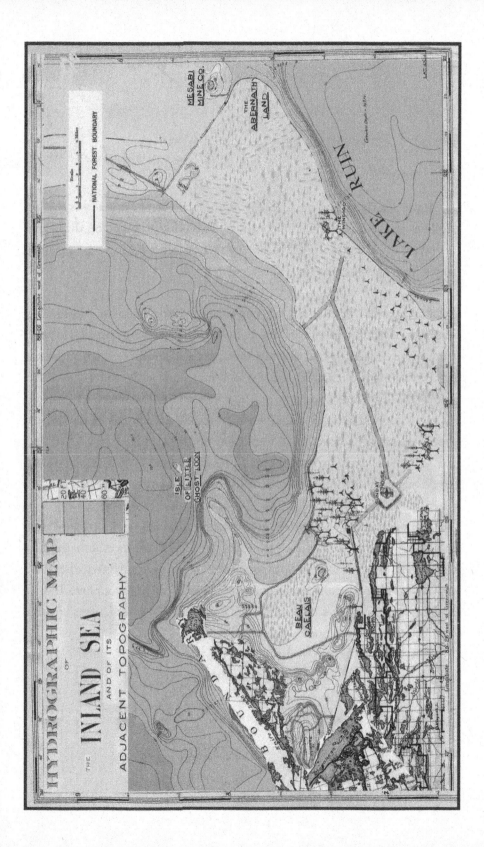

HYDROGRAPHIC MAP
OF
THE
INLAND SEA
AND OF ITS
ADJACENT TOPOGRAPHY

NATIONAL FOREST BOUNDARY

MESABI
MINE CO.

THE
ABERNATH
LAND

LAKE RUIN

ISLE
OF LITTLE
GHOST LOON

BEAU
CAILLAIS

A CROWN OF LOONS

1 December 2016

It was sleeting when the Caelais Co. Aquatic Patrol came across the Inland Sea in their ice-chopper motorboat. Two officers landed on the beach in front of our cabin around dusk, emergency lights flaring across glacial water. Snow just starting to fall.

Our island, Little Ghost, juts out of the Inland Sea on an unforgiving remnant of basalt and granite, birch, lichen, and blueberry brush. Isolated from the mainland, in bad weather it feels as far as another continent, when it is really only about a mile—maybe an hour's walk across the rocks, or the ice; by kayak a windy paddle.

That night, Dad was still at work on the Water Shuttle in the North Country, and my mother and I were alone on the island.

"Stay here, darling," she told me. "I'll send word."

"You're gonna leave me out here?" I yelled at the officers, at her.

It appeared so. I was sixteen, able to fend for myself—still, I wanted my mother to fight them. I'd heard stories of her fury. Marietta Abernathy was the kind to holler down a hall full of miners, to swing at men twice her size.

That night, she stood in the doorway of our cabin in a wool sweater and long underwear, with a crown of loons perched on her head, arms crossed over her chest. She was powerful, serene.

"Hi, Frank," she said to the older of the two.

"Mar," he said. "Sorry to see you like this."

"How's Linda?" she asked.

"You know," he said. "Missing our girl."[13]

....

13. See also: p. TK.

"Sorry to hear that," said my mother. "Tell her we send our love."

"I know you do," said Frank. "But listen, Mar—we gotta go."

"Is that so," she said. "And where is it that you're going?"

She didn't sound sarcastic—rather sincerely wondering, as if she were a curious bystander watching them speak to someone else. The officers looked at each other, back at her.

"Ah—well, to the jail, ma'am," the younger officer said.

"Can't take those birds with you, Marietta," said Frank.

She didn't move, so he reached.

The loons both crooned and flew, frantic like bats caught in a bathroom. One of them smashed into the star-loft glass and fell to the floor at my feet. The other escaped through the hole its mate had left behind. Wind off the Inland Sea swept in through the roof, and a rush of dried seed husks, snakeskins, feathers, and birch paper flew about our cabin, too.

It was sleeting still when they led her down the agate shoreline and onto the dock. The dying birches she had long cared for in our front yard shivered their naked branches behind us, and the old black pine leaned and moaned in the wind.

"It wasn't her," I kept saying to Frank Delacroix. "It couldn't have been her."

He looked uncomfortable, offered her his palm, and helped her into the middle of their boat.

"She was out here with us this whole time," I said, even though this was not entirely true and we all knew it. I opened my mouth to insist again, and my mother finally interrupted.

"Lena," she said. "Stop."

Her hair whipped around her face, sticking to the icy spray at her eyes, her neck. She was not wearing a coat, but did not appear to notice the cold.

"Ma," I said. "Tell them you didn't do it."

She ignored me, looked straight on toward the mainland. The engine roared up and they motored away.

When Dad got home from the North Country near midnight he turned right around and went to the Caelais Co. jail to talk to her, bring her some soup. I waited up for them in her rocking chair on the front porch, the injured loon curled in my lap. Only my nose was exposed, and as the wind pitched and the waves got higher, I fell asleep.

Dad woke me just as the sun was streaking across the Inland Sea again. The morning light was odd, weak and bitter.

"How's Ma," I asked.

"She's gone," he said.

"Where'd they take her? The Big City?"

"Not taken," he said. "Just gone. Guard says she escaped."

I stood up and the sleeping bag fell to the floorboards. I forgot about the bird I had been holding, and the loon warbled and wriggled from my hands, took off. Disappeared on one bloodied wing out over the water.

MY MOTHER HAD MANY NAMES

HOME | 48° 12' 57" NORTH & 90° 55' 23" WEST

Marietta Abernathy was the one she had been given.[14]

On the mainland in Beau Caelais, they called her the Loon Woman.[15]
The town Hydratic, meaning *water-crazy,*
the One Who Could Not Contain Her Tides.

Or rather:
the One Whose Hair was Perpetually Tangled and Speckled with Ash[16]
the One Whose Eyes Changed Color with the Seasons
the Land-Clumsy, the One Who Drowned, the One Who Stank of
    Algae[17]

She was the One Who Slept and Slept Under the Ice[18]
the One Whose Wild and Quiet Followed the Water[19]
the One Who Lost Control of Her Throat and Howled,[20] in public no
    less, and *how dare she*?

As the years overtook her, she became the Obsessive Collector of
    Ephemera

· · · · · · · · · · · · · · · · · ·

14. My mother may have married, but she never changed her surname, an act unheard
    of in our town. Still, it was surprising to no one, and yet another reason folks used to
    justify the boundaries they drew between themselves and her. *What's so wrong with
    Bailey?* they'd say. *Chance to make herself respectable. Make peace with the past.*
15. See p. TK, excerpt, *Snow Birch Bird: A Natural History of the North Country.*
16. See pp. TK.
17. See pp. TK.
18. See pp. TK.
19. See pp. TK.
20. See pp. TK.

the One Who Heard Water in the Walls
the One Who Dreamed the Fire and the Flood into Being[21]
the One Who Gathered Our Disappearing World, piece by piece, into her
  pockets and palms.

Most of all, though, the Loon Woman meant:
it was She Who Burst Pipes, Bones, Flood Barriers[22]
it was She Who Was Responsible.

After my mother disappeared into the World Below, there was no one left to defend her name. Folks on the mainland insisted, and that other form of her began to take shape in my memory. After she was gone, she became the Loon Woman to me, too. But in retrospect: I think we could also call her the Selkie Queen of the Inland Sea; the Banshee of Ruin Lake. Hecate of the Birches and the Boundary Islands.[23] How I wish I'd been able to see it was really:

She Who Remembered Everything.

I know now it is this version of her that bothered the town like a bruise.

. . . .

21. See p. TK.
22. See pp. TK.
23. See p. TK.

SOAKED AND MUDDY AND
BARELY TOILET-TRAINED

[excerpts, interview with Patrick Bailey]

You were about three, first time you got real curious.

One night she dreamt of something like drowning, and before she woke up—before I could wake her up—she'd burst the pipe to the kitchen sink. Next morning, we came down the star-loft stairs to a swamp that had filled up the cabin and spilled its way out into the yard.

The specimens she'd collected recently were not entirely lost to her Flooding, but many of them had escaped whatever containers she'd been keeping them in. The crawling algae she had been keeping had unfurled itself across the floors and up the walls. A school of dwarf sturgeon were trapped in a stockpot. Her last frost pine sapling had tipped over sideways on its root ball, and a pair of soggy ghost-nose bats had taken up residence in its boughs. Glass jars floated about the house like we were in a boat stalled in the doldrums, like we'd stumbled across every message ever lost to the sea in a bottle.

By half-past seven in the morning, she was crying. You were soaked and muddy, and only barely toilet-trained. The cabin started to smell of wet dog.

Mar was hungover from the dream—she spent most of that day wading around and wailing quietly while she tried to collect the things she'd Flooded; the following three days curled up in the empty bathtub basin with a sleep-mask over her eyes. I couldn't *both* clean the house *and* keep you from wandering off on the Inland Sea, so I convinced you it would be fun to bail sandcastle buckets of water out the front door. That occupied you for about twenty minutes, and then you got sick of stomping around in your galoshes. I had my head directly under the sink basin when you came and poked me in the gut.

"Papa," you said, very sternly. "Mama's zombie zoo is giving me the creeps."

Smacked my head against the pipe laughing. You were right, though. Gave me the creeps, too.

"Not funny," you said again, very sternly.

So I stopped laughing and put on my own stern face. I've known since you were very small to take you seriously when you are in a mood like this. You are your mother's daughter this way.

"Sorry, little girl," I said. "What's the trouble?"

"What happened to the hole?"

"What hole, Lena?"

"The one at the bottom of the lake," you said. "I saw it in Mama's dream, but now she can't find it."

THE WORLD BELOW, PART I

HOME | 48° 12' 57" NORTH & 90° 55' 23" WEST

20 June 2016—Six Months Until She Would Slip from the Jail Cell Window

My mother wanted to have a picnic.

"We never eat together," she said to Dad. "We never spend any time."

The next night, he came home early from the Water Shuttle with a string of sweet trout hanging from one hand, a basket of blueberries in the other.

"Where'd you find those?" she crooned, greedy, a handful of the small, tart fruit already in her mouth.

"Let's have a bonfire on the shore," he said.

And so my memory of it starts like this:

I am floating in the lake in a rubber tire; my mother swimming beside me in the water. A full moon shows every minor motion, the whole basin of the Inland Sea kaleidoscopic. It is the Solstice, an antiversary she celebrates in grim habit I do not understand at the time.

Dad sits on the rocky shore behind us—watchful, a fire of newsprint crackling in front of his heavy work boots. He roasts Spam dogs, rose hips; plays intermittently on his resonator. Its hammered steel body catches glimmers of the fire and throws light at me when Dad shifts his weight. The mainland is far away, muddled. A wash of stars spreads upward from the horizon. I remember the sound of the tide; the faint rumble of copper mine trains, their horns; the headlights of ash trucks on their way to the North Country.

I throw egg-sized agates into the lake for the Dogs to chase, but they are preoccupied with her, the Diving Bird. She wears a rubber mask that turns her eyes to planets, two swim fins painted like loon feathers. In her hand is an empty, sealed bottle labeled *pines & birches*.[24]

. . . .

24. I was not there when she held that bottle up above her head and trapped their eerie creaking, the wind of a summer thunderstorm whipping naked crown against root,

She dives and slips under without a ripple, returning after a minute. She dives again with specimen after specimen, does not return for almost too long. Each time she goes Below, she brings something down with her. When she resurfaces, her hands are empty.

Still not enough, she mumbles to herself.

I stay at the surface because I have what my mother calls *wet lungs.* Sometimes I can hear the water wheeze when I exhale. I struggle enough to catch my breath Above; I can't imagine staying underwater the way she does.

"Lena, come," she calls as she swims suddenly toward the shore. She stands knee deep and then bends, outstretched, one hand holding an empty jar, the other like a heron about to spear. A splash. A cry, triumphant. She holds up the jar, a small, rainbow-flecked fish spinning inside. It swims awkwardly, like a drunk, and one eye bulges from its head. When I look close I see it has an extra fin, a beating-heart tumor protruding from its belly.

"Two guesses," she says, "as to why they're born like this."

When the meal is ready Dad beckons us both in. He and I eat, but she hardly touches anything. Beside us in the scrabble and scrub grass are small treasures she caught in glass jelly jars that afternoon—a rosy cecropia moth flapping on a single wing; a cracked owl's egg; a floret of tiny wilted mushrooms the color of amber. She shoves a rose hip in her mouth and returns to the lake, dives again with a jar of blinking fireflies missing their antennae, a few limbs. She is gone ten seconds, then twenty, a minute, then two. My heart begins to pound in my chest—and then she surfaces again. The jar of fireflies is gone. She hauls herself ashore, loon-feather fins making her steps clumsy and loud. She leans over Dad, dripping lake into his hair while she kisses him. He looks up at her, at the moon.[25]

. . . .

but she had twice before tried to teach me how to capture sound in bottles. So far I have been unsuccessful. She says, *It's all right, Lena, it takes time,* so seriously that I believe we are able.

25. See also: pp. TK.

EVIDENCE

We made moon bones of you. Dark birds calling.

—Ellis Olsen

Ten thousand years of glaciation and geologic pressure cool at a latitude of 48° North. All manner of rock shifting in its basin—shale, granite, agate, taconite, dolostone, copper; all of it mixed in the great Mesabi Iron Range. Shoreline forest classified as *lower taiga, mixed deciduous*. Much of the Boundary Islands remains uninhabited except wayfarer camps left by those who regularly traverse. Five thousand cubic miles of water. One thousand feet down at its deepest point. Until the invention of the Diving Bell, the bottom was assumed an alien environment to human eyes. The myth of the Loon Woman would suggest otherwise.

—Snow Birch Bird: A Natural History of the North Woods

asthma / ˈæzmə / (n.) a disease of the lungs, due to a reactive narrowing of the bronchial tubes. Symptoms include labored breathing, hypoxemia, and hyperproduction of mucous. From the Greek ἄσθμα, or *shortness of breath, a panting*; probably related to ἄνεμος, meaning *wind*.

Fact and truth are not synonyms; nor are fiction, a lie, a myth their necessary opposite. Binaries be the scourge of us. I think I shall spend the rest of my days asking questions, as I fear I will feel unsettled and arrogant otherwise. For example: how the fuck do you plan to measure how human bias colors our understanding of the things we observe? How do our wildest, most beautiful, most ugly impulses alter how our brains analyze the sensory information our bodies receive? Are we capable of differentiating? Be curious, I beg of you.

—bell maree Baldwin, from the Artist's Statement for we are built for
more than war and fucking

Oh honey, don't go looking around there. It's not safe. Don't you know, they say the Devil lives in the wild rice on Ruin.

—Lidna Belkoop, adult services librarian, the Public Library of Caelais Co., Beau Caelais Branch

You queer? I don't let queers in my house.

—Rita Mae Mitchum, mother of Hugo

FOLKS FROM MESABI TOOK OUT ADVERTISEMENTS IN
THE *BEAU CAELAIS DAILY* CALLING HER

A WITCH

AND I SUPPOSE SHE WAS, OF A KIND:

A BENEVOLENT, WOOL-AND-PLAID-WEARING
APPARITION.

Deputy Ranger Ingrid Solberg-Black

MOON JUNKIES

THE BEAR & BIRD | 48° 3′ 6″ NORTH & 90° 30′ 18″ WEST

Aunt Bea bought the building that used to be the Windigo cheap from the Mesabi Mine Co. in 2002. It had been abandoned since the winter of 1999, when the Fire ran and burned everything around it for miles.

"I mean that's pretty eerie, right?" Aunt Bea says. "Folks think it's haunted. Guess I do, too … but that's what the spirits are for, I suppose."

They wink.

Years as the de facto House Mother for Wayward Teens at the Sunday House for Girls of Caelais County.[26] has given them an almost uncanny ability to crack dad jokes. It's likely this same history let them slowly transform the bar from an empty dive into a haven for an entirely different kind of underground company. Aunt Bea was the One Who Goes It Alone in euchre, the One Who Brews Moonshine (of wild rice and shriveling juniper berries) in Old Toilet Bowls. They told me stories of my grandmother,[27] whom they had loved and known well, before Ursa died giving birth to my mother. For me, at sixteen, the most influential thing about them was likely something that had been lifesaving for all the young folx they'd ushered through Sunday House: Beatrice Orleans was the One Who Was Never Shy of Warmth. All heat and soft flesh. Constantly hugging me, even when I was resistant. Laughing and laughing and laughing.

"I'm here for what, seventy-five, eighty years if I'm lucky?" they say.

"If I'm being selfish," I say, "I hope it's more like a hundred and twenty."

They raise an eyebrow.

. . . .

26. See Map. The name *Sunday House for Girls of Caelais County* is a remnant of its origins as a North Country Magdalene laundry. Aunt Bea says by the time they were the residential director, there were no gender restrictions—"Although," they say, "our forms still held to the binary."

27. See also: "The One Wherein Ursa Abernathy Climbed a Cliff"; "The One Wherein Ursa & Aunt Bea Got Married on Magnetic Rock"; "The One Wherein Ursa Abernathy Climbed Up on the Moon": pp. TK.

"I drink too much and sleep too little to make that," they say. "Sorry, kiddo. No time to waste. Seen enough shit."

Although it is now officially called the Bear & Bird, there are plenty of people in Beau Caelais who will forever refer to the bar by the Anishinaabe-mowin word for a cannibal spirit.

"Original owners were a Big City couple," they tell me. "Maybe they didn't know what it meant, or they just didn't think it would bring bad luck."

From the outside, the building could seem uninviting. The front glass was so thick with mildew it was hard to tell if there were any lights on in-side. Shingles sagged along the gutters, and the red cedar siding had long since turned the color of old embers. They had worked on the interior, though it too seemed less than it was—generic multicolored string lights, a jukebox, a popcorn machine, and an old, out-of-tune piano in the corner.

What turned the hard carved-maple booths cozy? How did the walls communicate they were far from the average hetero dive, if not by being flamboyant in color, leather studs, lipstick femmes, or flannel icons?

"We come to understand the energy of a place," Aunt Bea says. "Share it with each other, make it a home, cliché as it is. How many stories you think there are about a bar and its townies, its n'er-do-wells, its local damsels and drunks? Thousands. All of 'em the same, all of 'em different."

Like creation myths, it seems pressure and fear end in the same ways everywhere. By the time After the Collapse, the Bear & Bird had become the only place in all the North Country where queer folx could exist in the open, where femmes and boi-dykes and faeries and two-spirits and non-binary bodies were all congregating together for safety. The sign they'd painted above the bar says *Loon, Lunar, Lunatic—We're All Moon Junkies Here.*

I don't know if I'm a moon junkie, so I ask Aunt Bea.

"That's yours to define, honey," they say. "What'd'ya think?"

The Beau Caelais Daily

Come, Brothers, in my Flying
Machine - Up, We'll On Up,
Up We Go
Markets Abernathy

Premier Edition
The Island Sea: Today, sunny, a few afternoon clouds. High tan tonight, slightly more humid. Low 41. Tomorrow, sun then clouds. High

VOL. I...No. 1   Caelais County News for the North Country   **YESTERDAY'S NEWS TODAY**   www.beaucaelaistoday.com   *NIGHT EDITION*

ABERNATHY ESCAPES

COUNTY-WIDE SEARCH COMES UP EMPTY

Mitchum Death at Ruin Lake Ruled Homicide

ELSA BIRCH · BEAU CAELAIS

MARIETTA DROWNED ONCE AND CAME BACK.

YOUR MOTHER MAY BE WATER-HEARTED,

BUT I DOUBT EVEN SHE COULD DO THAT AGAIN.

Dad

GIRL SLIPS THROUGH HOLES LIKE OIL

HOME | 48° 12′ 57″ NORTH & 90° 55′ 23″ WEST

Local legend says all Abernathy women are born with skin the color of a glacier heart, and I was much like my grandmother Ursa, and my mother after her.

You ever have babies, my mother used to say, *they'll be born blue, too.*

We had all declined to breathe our first dry sips of oxygen until thrown out into the snow—Ursa on a drift of North Country glacier; my mother near the Mine in a blizzard; and myself on the ice of the Inland Sea itself, albeit in a bathtub. I think it was getting used to the idea we'd no longer live submerged in fluid that caused us to pause, to consider the new way of the world around us, before we opened our tiny mouths to howl. We are water-hearted. Hydratic.[28]

Although my grandmother's name was derived from the Great Bear in the stars,[29] Aunt Bea thinks of her a bit differently.

"That woman could just as easily been named for a mountain," they say. "Sturdy, cold, and stubborn as shit."

Our original familial property was not Little Ghost Loon, the small island of mixed taiga in the Inland Sea, but rather a quiet patch of birch and tall, wind-waving pines on the shores of Ruin Lake, two miles inland from Beau Caelais and the Inland Sea at the eastern edge of the Boundary Islands.[30] Ursa built a cedar cabin that my mother would later replicate

. . . .

28. **hydratic** / hī'drətɪk / (n.) one whose being is affected by water, or (adj.) water-crazy; see also: *hydracy* [hī'drəsē], (n.) to be lost or preternaturally afflicted by water and its presence; from the Greek ὕδωρ [*húdōr*] meaning *water*.

29. **arctic** [/ 'aːrktɪk / or / 'aːrtɪk /] (n.) from the Greek ἀρκτικός meaning *near the Bear, northern*, and that from the word ἄρκτος (*arktos*), meaning *bear*. Referring either to the constellation Ursa Major, most prominent in the North Country sky, or to the constellation Ursa Minor, which contains Polaris, the guiding North Star itself.

30. See Map.

twice[31] with her bare hands, the star-loft where we slept intended to keep us *honest with our small selves*, as she liked to say, *here amidst all these celestial bodies.* Both women planted seasonal gardens—rice and blueberries, nettle, sweet peas, rose hips, trout lily, fungi—that along with the trout and small mammals they caught kept them fed spring through autumn. The Collapse[32] brought that to an end before I was able to carry on the tradition.

I cannot determine how Ursa came to lay claim to the property on Ruin—if she'd inherited it, squatted, bought it as a homestead from the government, or won it in a poker game off a neighbor. Perhaps she stole it outright. Perhaps she never owned it at all. Just adjacent was the acquisition office of the Ruin Lake branch of the Mesabi Mine Co.[33] Between them, along the shoreline and around the Abernathy property in a loop, there lay buried a contested iron ore deposit.[34]

. . . .

31. First time Above, on the Isle of Little Ghost Loon. See also: p. TK. The cabin was a small A-frame of birch and dead pine, and it is, was, and will ever be the only structure erected there—the water and the wind are just too wild for anything much to last. She was just turned seventeen, eight months pregnant, and alone, except for her dogs and the loon pair nested there on the island, when she cut and laid the wide weathered floorboards by hand. A week and a few hours after she was done building, I was born into a claw-foot tub filled with melting Inland Sea ice. The lake only just cracking open for the spring. She would fill the shelves and rafters with caught light, found objects; later, she would dismantle the roof and the door and then even the floor, out from under our feet in pieces. The glass loft at the peak she forged and tempered herself; later, she would paint maps on that invisible barrier with her fingers and tell me stories about the stars; later, she would splinter it with a fist, so desperate to break out, to make her way toward the moon. The stove and the rocking chair and the microscope—all of it she rowed across the water so that we would have a home; later, she would let Dad help her keep us safe and fed; later, she would leave me, again and again. The cabin Above is gone now, but I remember the walls breathed like giant bellows in rhythm with the tide. I don't sleep well, without that keen and creak.

32. What will be the first of a series in the Anthropocene, here referring to a biome-level event in the North Country, marked by catastrophic loss of biodiversity via trophic cascade and decreasing water access/quality.

33. See Map.

34. A stretch of land desirable because its stand of old pine, cedar, and birch had remained intact, while the timber companies had cleared out everything else in front of the mining trucks. Vibrant, healthy forest on the Abernathy land was ringed like a doughnut hole by dead and useless soil.

According to microfilms at the Beau Caelais Public Library, Ursa staged a protest deemed *illegal trespass on company property* and was found three days later, dead in the snow.[35] Nine months after meeting and fucking a young Hunter from the North Country and accidentally getting pregnant, she had apparently gone into labor in the middle of a sleet storm, wandered out in what the Caelais Co. coroner referred to as *a blind, hormonal rage,* where she bled until her body was empty of both life and her tiny newborn daughter, my mother, Marietta. The slash across her midsection would seem to indicate another's involvement, but no investigation was ever initiated, as far as I can figure. My requests for police records re this matter were returned, unopened. People say the Hunter found my mother in a drift, blue as Ursa had been. How she survived I do not know, but I imagine her first moments: purple-mouthed, bawling.

Aunt Bea tells me my maternal grandfather stuck around long enough after Ursa died to teach my mother how to tie her shoes, how to forage berries and catch walleye and boil beans in a dented aluminum pot, but soon he claimed that she was haunting him.

"Before he abandoned her, he used to tell anyone who would listen she was possessed," they say. "Tells me Marietta *fills our house with cups and buckets of water. Piles ice up in the middle of the floor and it keeps! Girl slips through holes like oil into concrete. Disappears, turns up again without sense. Something queer about 'er.* Can you imagine? Big man afraid of a six-year-old, for fuck's sake."

Around the time Marietta had her seventh birthday, he shot, dressed, and smoked one of the few remaining moose to be found in the North Country, hung it in the rafters of the cabin above a stepladder that was just tall enough for her to reach the meat from, then disappeared south down 61. Being good Lutherans, his neighbors in Beau Caelais were suspicious of the Abernathy women because they had never come to church, and

. . . .

35. See p. TK.

as they were already inclined to be terrified of God, they left judgment of my mother's father to his maker and did not intervene.

Social services took custody of her, and for a time she stayed at Sunday House for Girls of Caelais County. Records show she struggled with *disciplinary issues*, but that the social worker—one Mx. Beatrice Orleans—took special care to make certain she felt loved. Sunday House records of my mother's whereabouts stopped when she ran away, in the winter of 1998, age fifteen.

We took the girls constellation-watching at the marina this evening, writes Aunt Bea in my mother's file. *Nobody saw her, but Marietta must have walked out onto the ice. Police came, searched until sunlight. Watched for her weeks after. Eventually we figured she had fallen in, or run away. She was near old enough to be considered a legally emancipated minor, so we've rescinded the Missing Person report.*

"To be honest," says Aunt Bea, "I wasn't worried. I knew she could take care of herself. But I was employed by the County at the time, had to obey mandatory reporting rules. I figured she'd get in touch when she was ready."

There are neither official reports nor anecdotes I can find that would indicate she had been seen in the vicinity that whole winter or the following spring, but in truth she was in the process of moving back to Ursa's cabin on Ruin. In a photo of the property from the *Beau Caelais Daily*, the glass in the windows had cracked, the garden was in disarray, overcome by wild yarrow, fireweed, and a corner of the roof had collapsed under a thunderstruck cedar. A black bear was rumored to have been seen habitually plundering the fruit that grew in the yard, though I cannot confirm this. People began to wonder if the girl had starved or frozen to death somewhere out in the woods, if she had perhaps drowned herself in the lake out of grief, melancholy teenage angst.

You Abernathy women always seem trouble, folks always say. *Someone shoulda kept a closer eye.*

The summer after my mother had turned sixteen, Mesabi made plans to begin excavation on the Abernathy property. In the months previous, the

World As It Was had disappeared. Beau Caelais became a boomtown, all iron money and timber.[36] Believing Ursa's land to be abandoned, the Mine took the last known deed to court and eventually won custody of the land from the State. They brought out their cranes and their trucks. The geologist came with his topographical maps and pointed at the men in steel-toed boots, who started marking white dots in paint.

Frank—Francis Delacroix II, Caelais Co. Aquatic Patrol officer, former site chief at the Ruin Lake Branch of the Mesabi Mine Co.—had agreed to meet with me after my mother disappeared from the jail cell. Tells me he feels obligated to explain what he knows.

On the day when the Mine was to begin digging its central line, the workmen arrived ready to bulldoze the cabin.

"Now I guess she'd looped a length of chain around her waist," he says. "Strung it to the door of the cabin, around one of the pines we were about to cut. Bolted it shut with a series of locks. Polite as can be, she says, *Could you move your trucks, the pipelines? I feel them pressing down on me.*

My men cut the chains easy with a pair of railroad-tie clippers, and I asked the young one—Ellis Olsen, six foot four, broad as an ox just like his father—to carry her up to the road, keep her outta the way. He grabbed her up like a fawn in the grass, but she didn't go easy. Kicking and screaming, all limbs wheeling. She was a slim, athletic girl, your mother. Before he could manage to fit her into the cab of his truck, she bit him twice: once in the shoulder, the second time aiming for his neck. She succeeded in tearing

· · · · · · · · · · · · · · · · · ·

36. And owned mainly by two families—Ole Ironsen of Ironsen & Associates, and Arthur Mitchum, of the Mesabi Mine Co. In Beau Caelais, a tight-knit town, it is these two bloodlines with more power than others: the Ironsens, Kings of Resource and Industry, meaning timber, iron ore, and the watershed of the Inland Sea; the Mitchums, whose churchgoing, blue-collar-workingman appearance belies their ties to a thriving black market and a lack of moral conviction or empathy, through which they profit from every tangible vice. My mother always insisted we Abernathy women were above them, that we were tangential to their world because we existed in our own. Unfortunately for both of us, only the first part was ever even partially true.

off a bit of earlobe, enough to make him drop her. Then she ran toward Ruin. Dove in without a sound."

Frank says they stood around and waited, watching for movement in the underbrush, on the rippling water, twitching at every squirrel rustle and every flopping fish. When she did not surface, they restarted their machines. The land, the birches, the original cedar cabin—all of it disappeared in less than an hour.

"After that, folks at the Windigo[37] started whispering she was a reincarnation of your grandma. That's when they started callin' her a witch."

In many ways, it seems they might have been right. Ursa was rumored to have had ephemerally colored eyes whose irises changed hues with the season, and although my mother's were generally a shade of dark green-violet uncommon in the North Country, I remember watching her eyes gather flecks of icy gray in the winter, shift to teal as the trees blossomed and the lakes thawed and the migrating birds returned to flirt. They'd flame out in bits of hazel and honey-orange by autumn, lose their color almost entirely like the glow of moonlight on ice by the turn of the New Year. Mine do the same, though I must look in mirrors to notice.

Like my mother and grandmother, I too share their short, strong legs, their small but perky pear-shaped breasts. Toxic slurry from the Mesabi Explosion made it so I could never swim in Ruin Lake, but people say they both loved to do so bare-ass naked, regardless of the weather. They were both fond of imitating birds in public, despite the looks they received from strangers, and they both loved to sing to their dogs, who always howled back in curdling harmony. According to all the local men they had rejected, both had slutty, lesbian tendencies. Though Ursa had slept with the Hunter and borne my mother, I can't speak to her proclivities or attractions other than a few stories Aunt Bea will sometimes share if they've had one too

. . . .

37. See also: wiindigoo / wiindigoow- / (n.) according to the *Dictionary of the Anishinaabe*, meaning: a cannibal monster that often appears in winter, especially during storms or bitter cold; a malevolent formerly human spirit transformed by violent greed or selfishness; from proto-Algonquin *wi·nteko·wa*;

many whiskeys. My mother was barely even pubescent when words like *whore, dyke,* and *cunt* started to drift in her general direction. Like Ursa too she would come to physical harm when she dared to battle with the Mine.

When Mesabi did not immediately agree to return the deed to her property and, in fact, continued to scrape copper and iron ore from the earth, to foul the water in Ruin with unending sour liquid leaching through the soil, my mother took to walking once daily to the Windigo. Rather than drinking too much cheap whiskey and passing out in a ditch or a stream on the way home, she harangued visitors from outside the building with inflammatory signs and a bullhorn like a teenage North Country version of Mother Jones. No one knew where she was living—in a tree fall near Ruin, perhaps, or a cave nearby at the Falls, an abandoned dam over the border.

"She'd get uncomfortable, real close," says Aunt Bea, "plaster maps of proposed sites too near the Inland Sea for her liking to every truck, motorcycle, and man."

Others claim she had suggested rude things to them about the way the watershed would smell if the ore was released from the earth. She set up a folding card table in the parking lot and advertised a *homemade, secret family recipe* of lemonade that was later determined to be slurry she had collected from another nearby Mesabi site after it had been closed and *cleaned.*

"Few of the miners started to complain," says Aunt Bea. "But there were other folks who believed her. It was then she got the idea."[38]

. . . .

38. See "The Paper Moon Menagerie," pp. TK.

SO MUCH LIKE SALT

My mother has been disappearing in rising and falling water since I was very young. Like the story Dad told me about waking up to a broken pipe and a swamp dreamed into life on the inside of our cabin, I never caught the Flood while it was happening,

only afterward

when I could see where she'd over-

flowed or dissolved.[39] What I called her Times of Missing are fuzzy now: I'd wake one morning and she was No Longer Near. She'd be gone for a few days, a week at a time. When she burst, the water rose up; when she calmed, the water went down. But despite her best efforts to hide it, she left proof behind. There were puddles on the floor or wet footprints toward the door. The water stains on the walls or the rocks around the cabin, at the small of my wrists or the inside of Dad's collarbone were always telling—that fine residue looked so much like salt, but as it came from the Inland Sea, it tasted of   limestone and whitefish.

Dad and I did the best we could. The three of us had lived out on Little Ghost alone my whole life. We had visitors (other than Aunt Bea) exactly twice in my memory, both of which were the Caelais County Aquatic Patrol come to take reports on or searching for my Missing mother. If we wanted anything, we had to conjure it from the air, find it floating somewhere in the Inland Sea, or go to the mainland. When it was my mother that we needed, there weren't many places to go.

The night before my tenth birthday she disappeared and didn't come

---

39. In retrospect, these Floods align with moments of deep rage or grief, though I did not understand this at the time. See also: *I Am Dreaming of the Women Beneath: The Collected Journals of Marietta Abernathy.*

back for a month.[40] When she finally returned, she appeared on the shore-line beside our cabin as if she'd fallen out of the sky. She was Gone and then Not Gone.

I remember:

it was dinner   I was calling for the Dogs   I turned at the sound of her voice.

My dear girl, she said. *It's so good to see your face.*

Her hair was tangled, she was wearing one sock and no pants, and there was some kind of ash smeared across her face. She cocked her head, smiled slight so the dimples appeared in her cheeks. Bruises marled across her thighs, the palms of her hands.

What happened? I asked.

She stared at her own body as if she were surprised, untethered from herself.

Huh, she said. *Those weren't there before.*

You missed my birthday, I said.

When was your birthday? she asked.

Where were you? I asked, only half curious.

The World Below, she'd said, *now let's go eat.*

As if that was enough explanation.

. . . .

40. I do not remember much of this time other than the dreams I had, wherein her face often appeared to me in mirrors, puddles of melting ice, once at the bottom of an indoor swimming pool partially covered in a giant yellow tarp.

A SMALL BOAT MOVING TOWARD THE NORTH COUNTRY

2 December 2016

Late afternoon the day after she disappeared from the jail, the Caelais Co. Wilderness Service called off their search. A fog had settled over the Inland Sea and swallowed the horizon. The blizzard had shuttered the whole county—drifts of unprecedented height on the roads, icy rain that made walking dangerous, especially near the water. Still, the cops wanted nothing but to erase she'd ever been in their custody at all.

"Come get her shit," said the officer at the jail over the shortwave. "Crazy cunt wants to be out in that, be my guest. Likely she's frozen anyway. Got what's coming."

I begged Dad to let me go along. He didn't fight long, knew I'd probably have snuck after him if he'd left without me anyway.

"Stay right behind," he said. "Watch where you step."

And so we dredged across the land bridge on our snowshoes, one foot slow in front of the other.

The cell where she had been kept was a small, dirty-gray room on the third floor of the Beau Caelais City Hall. A single-paned window at one corner looked out over the lake, sealed and fused shut. The glass had not been broken; from that height, a drop would have broken her knees at the very least.

"How, exactly, did she escape?" Dad asked.

The officer shrugged as he bent with a sponge and a bucket, a smirk crossing his face.

"Pipes burst when the temperature dropped," he said, and pointed to a white water line I hadn't noticed along the wall, a dust of residue on the warped wood floors. He scrubbed and scrubbed, but my mother would not wash off. "Whole building flooded. Door probably came loose on the hinges."

"But you don't know," said Dad.

"Nah," said the officer.

"Nobody here on watch?"

"Nah," said the officer.

"Where were you? Where was anybody?"

The officer licked his chapped, scaly lips.

"We was out buryin' my nephew."

He paused his scrubbing and puffed out his chest so we would see *Mitchum* stitched next to his badge.[41] He stared at Dad and Dad stared back at him, and finally his eyes shifted over to mine, where they stuck. I looked down.

"Where's Frank?" asked Dad.

"Out," said the officer.

"Out?" I asked.

"Out," said the officer in a tone that said *there will be no more clarification*.

"I'll have her stuff now," Dad said. "C'mon, Lena."

The officer gave me the bag of her belongings—the wool sweater, a pair of heavy boots, a toothbrush, and a handful of speckled black-and-white feathers.

"She's not wearing any shoes?" I asked.

The officer shrugged again.

"You know as good as anybody else, girl," he said to me, then spiraled his middle finger at his temple.

We left the station around midnight, walked home through the snow. In the hour it took us to trudge back over the lake, we didn't say a word between us. He pretended my keening was part of the wind. When he fell to his knees,

. . . .

41. Hugo Mitchum's father, Arthur, had three brothers, Abel, Arlo, and Anders, all of whom were Caelais Co. sheriff's deputies. I could neither distinguish which of these men was which, nor remember which of them was on duty at the county jail when we came to collect my mother's belongings. Their pinched, red faces blur forgettably in the way men of a certain age and demeanor often do.

I kept going, head down. Back home, we lay down in front of the fire to get warm, too tired to climb the stairs to the star-loft. I felt damp and the cabin seemed full of water, full of my mother. Dad rolled onto his stomach and slept.

I tried. I tried, but it was too still without her around, and my accordion lungs started to sing in my chest.

Just breathe, I thought. *Count the constellations.*

Ursa Major. *Breathe.* Corvus, the Lynx. *Breathe.* Cassiopeia. *Breathe.* The Pleiades, the Dog Star. *Breathe. Breathe.* Open-mouthed, I sucked in air. *Breathe.* Wheeze. *Breathe.* Wheeze. *Breathe.*

There was a brief break in the snow, right around three, and the whole sky unfurled in the star-loft glass above me. It was then that a light flickered across the walls of the cabin, through the front lakeside window and over the door, the star-loft, the bathtub. Light ran, and then it was gone.

I stared into the dark, thinking I'd imagined it.

Breathe. Wheeze. *Breathe.*

A few moments passed, but then the light came again through the window, bounced, and ran.

A third time, brighter, more like a lantern.

And then there was a knock.

I jumped up and opened the door, looked out into the dark. The beach in front of me was abandoned. I clutched my sleeping bag to my chest, narrowed my eyes. Stared out farther, at the ice chunks crunching across the surface of the Inland Sea, at the moon glinting off the ice.

It was her headlamp bobbing away from the shore, just above the water, that caught my eye. The glow hovered and swung, pointed up into the sky above my head, and then drifted out onto the waves.

Ma, I muttered first, as if she were standing next to me. I left the door wide open to the lake and went out into the wind, sweaty hair sticking to my scalp. I saw the outline of a small boat moving toward the North Country.

It must have been hard rowing, slow going against the current. I started shouting. Her headlamp swung back into my eyes, and I shut them—just for a moment—but when I opened them again it was dark.

The boat was gone. Just shy of the waterline, she'd left a steamer trunk—brass rivets, leather strops, peeling blue paint on wood—one snap unhinged so the seal hovered not quite shut.

THE PAPER MOON MENAGERIE[42] stamped on the side in black block letters.

I bent, pulled at the strops, opened the lid. My eyes drifted over a familiar collection of jars and thin paper packages: the skin of a snake; a handful of teeth; a small diorama of injured insects; several seasons' worth of collected seeds waiting for a time, a place where they might be able to grow. Several hand-bound leather journals.[43] A cassette tape.[44] An apothecary bottle filled with ash.[45] A collection of newspaper clippings, some of them yellowed or water-stained and starting to smudge.[46] Photographs, and several pieces of frenzied collage art I knew she had made at her desk in the star-loft.[47] But the largest object was a blue glass ball, inside of which was a live, keeling loon. Its wing was visibly bloodied, even in the dark.

Over and over, the bird called to its mate—eerie wind, a warning horn.

I turned the ball gently in my hands and looked for a doorway, a seal.

How did she get the bird in here? I thought. *How is it still breathing?*

At the very bottom of the trunk, there was a paper bird, identical to

. . . .

42. For a partial list of contents, see p. TK.
43. See also: *I Am Dreaming of the Women Beneath: The Collected Journals of Marietta Abernathy.*
44. See *Soundtrack*, p. TK.
45. Folks talk about the Insomnia of Ashes, c. 1999–2000, as if it was a surreal, unsettling dream they could not wake from. Beau Caelais was bitter in thirst. Everyone had been making do with too little for too long; by the end they were less inclined to be generous, to see themselves in their neighbors' needs. They pulled their children from school, lied about the stockpiles they kept in their cellars. Everything in town closed down for lack of supplies. The poorest families could afford neither to import necessities nor to abandon their homes and move southward, so a growing crowd spent their days gathering trapped mussels and carp from tidal pools; the driftwood that had been left behind for winter wood piles. See also: pp. TK.
46. See pp. TK.
47. See pp. TK.

the loon in the globe. Just like the notes she used to leave for me to find as a child, when she would disappear for days at a time.

I unfolded the wings, the beak, the long, graceful spine.

A letter from my mother.

PAPER LOONS

1 DEC.

Lena: We'll all lose everything if you're not careful, so listen close.

Write everything down,
take pictures,
make records;   witness.
Capture as much as you can in ink and color and sound.

Then bring it down here, to the World Below. This is how you save us. This is how we remember the World As It Was.

I used to know but I fear I've maybe lost my way. You'll have to finish what I started. If you don't, it'll all be black and cold, Lena, baby. No light, no water, no more growing living things.

I've gone down to be with the Women   Beneath. To keep safe. Come find me when you can.

Close your eyes and see yourself between layers. Speak to me through the air, if you need to. I'll hear you, darling girl.

Make fluid millennia, memory.
Everything can be a doorway.

                    Everything can be a hole . . .

EVIDENCE

We paint the World Below
with our bruises, opal-blue and mint   green, yellow like dandelion pollen
we make   snow of cut paper
            skin, blood on our fingertips, wrists
we stitch our   hearts together with
glue,   all that pink milk spilled
                when our   limbs peeled open like citrus,
                            split, no hesitation
                            so sticky sweet and sour
        —the Women   Beneath

Three months before you were born, late December, an explosion at the
Mesabi copper mine on Ruin sparked dry piled wood at the Ironsen timber
mill, and spilled slurry into the lake. Fire caught. All that tinder pine and
birch of the Boundary forests. Miles of cultivated and wild growth alike.
In retrospect, seems like that was a moment of war. Certainly brought the
Insomnia of Ashes.[48] Almost seventeen years later, folks still talk in metaphors, hushed voices. They're every one of 'em afraid to speak too loud and
bring it back to life. You've seen those photos from the *Daily*. According to
Frank, the Mitchum kid was the one on the schedule, but it was Ellis Olsen
on watch at Ruin that night. When the rescue crew found him three days
after the flames went down, he was terribly burned and half-blinded, his
right eye turned white.

    —Deputy Ranger Ingrid Solberg-Black, Caelais Co. Wilderness Service

My boy? My boy was good. You don't know. You don't know. Just leave.
Leave. You're not welcome here. Leave us be—

                        —Mrs. Elin Ironsen, mother of Ellis

. . . .

48. The autumn and winter seasons following the Ruin Lake fire of 1999; see also: *Snow
    Birch Bird: A Natural History of the North Country*, p. TK.

Boys will be boys, right, but that Mitchum kid was hard to handle. Everybody in town knew Ellis Olsen was soft. Big gentle man, big gentle hands. What does it matter? Doesn't matter. I think he was sweet on one of the fishermen once, but I never knew him to act. Nobody would've cared, except Hugo Mitchum. Boys on the Mesabi crews say he pushed and prodded while they were working, got belligerent, pushed more. At the Windigo a couple days before, I heard 'em arguing. Ellis said somethin' about leaving well enough alone. *You don't come along*, Hugo says, *I'mma tell everybody you fuck moose in rut*. Had a way of speaking so you heard. I wasn't the only one close enough that I had to turn away to pretend. And nobody spoke up, myself included.

—Frank Delacroix, Caelais Co. Aquatic Patrol, retired site chief, Mesabi Mine Co., Ruin Lake Branch

The dialectic of trauma gives rise to complicated, sometimes uncanny alterations of consciousness, which George Orwell, one of the committed truth-tellers of our century, called "doublethink" and which mental health professionals, searching for calm, precise language, call "dissociation." It results in protean, dramatic, and often bizarre symptoms ...

—Judith Herman, *Trauma and Recovery*, p. xx.

Subject reported to have been seen in vicinity of body discovery site [see report by Deputy Rgr. Solberg-Black] sometime between hours of 20:30 and 02:00. Subject's reported residence, a condemned Mesabi Co. shed deemed unfit for human habitation, lies approx. three hundred yards northeast of location of body discovery site.

OFF. FRANCES DELACROIX II: Ellis, you know you can't be staying here. We got a room you can stay at in the station for the winter. Or your family, your sisters. Surely one of them can put you up on a couch.

ELLIS OLSEN: We left her in the lily-weeds. Mud and moon bones.

DELACROIX: No, Ellis. Hugo. Your old friend Hugo—Ingrid found him last night. Did you see who left him there?

OLSEN: Mud and moon bones.

DELACROIX: Yeah, in the mud. There was a full moon last night ... Did you see anyone with Hugo?

OLSEN: Mud on my hands, made ash of my eye.

DELACROIX: You—you have mud on your hands? I know you can't see too well, but did you see Hugo last night?

OLSEN: Moon bones in the lily-weeds. We left her in the lily-weeds.

DELACROIX: Who's her, Ellis? Look, you gotta focus. Listen to me.

OLSEN: Dark birds calling.

DELACROIX: We should get you to a doctor. You don't look so good. When's the last time you had anything to eat? Had a proper bath, a bed? Let me take you to the station. Call your sister.

OLSEN: The Devil lives in the wild rice on Ruin.

DELACROIX: Who's the Devil, Ellis?

OLSEN: Dark birds calling now.

HE NEVER SLEEPS OR SHOWERS

RUIN LAKE | 48° 12' 09" NORTH & 90° 52' 29" WEST

Like all slightly odd folx in small, gossipy towns, Ellis Olsen was the Boogeyman of Beau Caelais.

"He's Lost, I guess," says Dad when I ask how he came to be that way. "Not something for you to worry about, kiddo."

He was the One Who Survived but Not Quite; the One Who Showed the Fire on His Face; the One Who Haunted the Mainland. There were rumors he was actually some kind of zombie my mother had resurrected, though she suffered no fools who asked after this, my sixteen-year-old-self included. Kids at school used to call him the Ghost with No Eyes, even though he had one that saw just fine. Same kids said he'd traded his soul to the Devil for magic vision in the bad one, an orb bleached white like a moonstone popped in his socket. I've no idea what Ellis Olsen may have bartered or with whom, and until my mother disappeared into a blizzard that winter night in 2016, I'd had no plans to ask him.

After the Fire, to go *into the woods* meant to travel through a landscape of ghosts—pine stumps, weathered moose racks and disarticulated spines, the skeletons of cabins internally open to the sky. Even the air seemed to agree, and the wind off the lake made visible eddies of ash. Few dared cross into that wasteland; certainly the only one who dared live there was Ellis Olsen.

He was barely older than my mother, younger than Dad by a few years, but his hair had turned stark white, and seemed constantly speckled with ash. The scars on his mouth pulled at the skin of his eyes, and the scar tissue on his right hand had reached and hardened toward the elbow until it hobbled the entire arm like a lame wing. Though he slept in a shack he'd built of Mesabi remaindered tin, driftwood, and half-burned branches, it was so decrepit he'd basically been living outside for sixteen years. During the day, he wandered the road from Ruin to Beau Caelais and back, jabbering at passersby. At night, he wandered the woods alone, scavenging off the remains of roadkill, owl pellets.

He never sleeps, folks always said. *Or showers.*

The latter was almost certainly true—a foul, exhausted stink emanated from him as if he had been cooked and left out in the sun. If I ever mentioned him to my mother, she'd act as if I had not said anything at all.

TINY, SUBTLE APOCALYPSES

[excerpts, interview with Deputy Ranger Ingrid Solberg-Black]

Part science project, part art installation. Whatever it was, it was hopeful. Sisyphean, but hopeful. Ballsy even—or should we say ovarian? She'd hate being called ballsy. I hate it, too, but I hate more how the bravest person in all of Beau Caelais was a sixteen-year-old girl.

In ranger training, we had to take taxonomy, botany, soils, limnological surveys. I would not classify what she was doing as scientific exactly—but maybe that was the point. After the Collapse all that knowledge was basically obsolete, and we humans are very fucking resistant to change. Scrambled to maintain our status quo when there was no status quo left, making it worse by the minute, as positive feedback loops tend to do. Not your mother, though.

People started bringing things to her. Specimens, I mean. The Mine did their best to persuade everyone in Beau Caelais she was a kook, but some were starting to see what she had been ranting on come to pass, and their fear of association with the Abernathy was lesser than their fear of the tiny, subtle apocalypses visiting us—one lost frog or bloom or birdsong at a time.

. . . .

49. See Map.

THE PAPER MOON MENAGERIE[50]

_____

108 OLD SHORE ROAD[51]

Thank you for visiting. Archiving our disappearing world is an urgent communal endeavor, and I appreciate your contribution. Any and all specimens are welcome. There is no danger of repetition. Yours are unique and alone in existence.

Examples of Previous Donations

- handfuls of silt from your favorite lake bed
- feathers from the heron you struck with your truck's windshield, or the heron itself, living or dead
- weeds from your garden
- the pests you pluck from your brassicas and your peas
- dropped moose racks
- the waters of intermingling tributaries in the Boundary Islands (+/- 8 oz; glass only, thank you)
- a net full of yearling gray jays or herring
- herds of winter ticks stuffed with moose blood
- fresh or moldy pine needles, birchbark, or maple leaves
- asphalt from Highway 61
- iron, mica, dolomite, taconite, or limestone

. . . .

50. Reproduced here from the original, which she had typewritten on paper too thin to handle, c. spring 1999.
51. See Map.

- the rust on the bottom of your boat's bailing bucket
- your last jar of serviceberry jam
- fish jelly
- wolfsbane; wolf's fur, wolf's scat; wolf pups
- ashes
- seeds of aster
- bulb of trout lily
- rut of bear, tuft of lynx ear

Please select the most appropriate container(s) for your specimen(s), and leave two forms of detailed description regarding its/their appearance and meaning in whatever manner you so choose, though one record must be a verbal recording using the Moon Telephone handset. Include whatever sensory or experiential detail you deem imperative to its/their full preservation, including but not limited to: physical attributes, seasonal fluctuations, (dis)pleasing scents, locative or contextual information, geographic or demographic statistics, emotions, memories, irrational fears or manic exaltations you may have experienced surrounding said specimen, abstract metaphors, vocal imitations, and/or synesthetic associations with sound, color, texture, and sight.

M. Abernathy

The Beau Caelais Daily

VOL. I., No. 1   Caelais Count, News by the Night Edition   **YESTERDAY'S NEWS TODAY**   www.beaucaelaistoday.com   *NIGHT EDITION*

WINDIGO TRANSFORMED

LOCAL BREWPUB NOW QUEER HOTSPOT

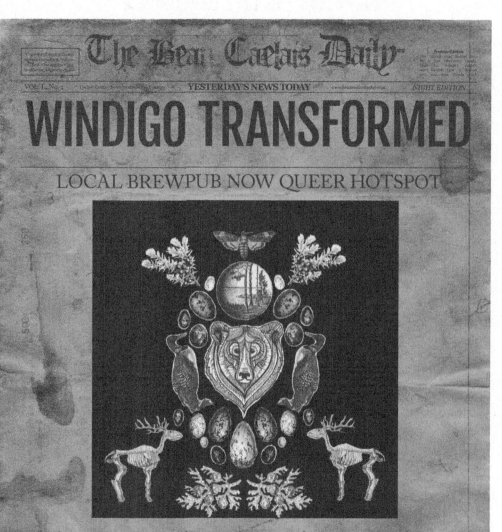

Orleans Renames Miner Dive for Deceased Lover

LISA BIRCH · BEAU CAELAIS

For thirty-four years, elders of the Rain Lake Band of Caelais Co. have objected to the name of a local mining establishment, known for the North Woods native cannibal spirits collectively named. But when the Mesabi Mining Co. sold the building and the business rights to local social worker Beatrice Orleans, she decided to change the reputation of the location to commemorate her deceased former partner and Beau Caelais native, Ursa Abernathy. "The *Bear & Bird* will be welcoming to all comers, most importantly those who have felt

marginalized or unsafe in traditional pub spaces in the North Country before. It was important to Ursa that folks be able to dance, laugh, sing, and drink in comfort, and her dream that all queer folk would one day have the ability to express themselves in public as they would in private without fear of retribution, harassment, or isolation." Orleans says the Caelais County community of LGBTQ, non-binary, two-spirit, and gender-non-conforming individuals is much higher than recent census data would imply, partially because a recent string

of suspected hate-crime graffiti attacks has reinforced the power of a small but vocal minority of community members who utilize bigoted rhetoric to intimidate their neighbors. "It's a shame, really, because I think folks up here in the North Country generally believe in the idea of live-and-let-live. Kindness and communion. Anybody likes to listen to a little birchbark blues is welcome in here. Come as you are, stay as you're able. I'm brewin' a special stout for the winter solstice - Ursa loved bourbon and chocolate around the new year."

HECATE OF THE BIRCHES &
THE BOUNDARY ISLANDS

HOME | 48° 12' 57" NORTH & 90° 55' 23" WEST

When I tell Aunt Bea I am reading about mythology, drawing lines between that old world and ours, they raise an eyebrow at me.

"Whose stories?" they ask.

The truth is I had not thought about this; I'd merely started with books marked *Myths* in the library.

"Start with that question," they tell me. "Whose voice are you listening to? Whose voice is telling the tales?"

So I search for my mother.

Five things:

1. Marietta Abernathy mirrors the Greek Queen of the Witches.[52]

2. They share an inherent relationship to boundaries or edges; knowledge of herbology; an inclination to mirror the moon and its phases; affection for snakes; a slightly obsessive affiliation with the underworld.

3. Other comparisons: a preference for nighttime; the ominous bearing of torches; the collecting of flora and fauna; the conjuring of life where there had been none.

4. I would name Marietta Abernathy less patient. More prickly. She never had nor would wait for anyone. Still, the Women   Beneath flocked to her as if she were some kind of constellation they'd discovered, a light to

. . . .

52. **Hecate** hɛkəti | Ἑκάτη | *Hekátē*, (n.) from the Greek *hekas*, meaning *far off.* Literally the Far-Reaching One, or One who works from afar.

lead them toward safe passage. The Goddess of Keys led women to the dock that would take them across the River Styx, but my mother had no interest in handing anyone over to Hades, much less any mortal man in a boat.

5. I suppose if my mother is Hecate, then my grandmother would be the Titan goddess Asteria, she of falling stars and oneiromancy,[53] who once turned herself into a quail and leapt into the sea in order to avoid fucking Zeus.

Aunt Bea agrees with this reading of them.

"Well, if Ursa wasn't a queer bird," they say with a snort, "I ain't never heard of one. Who's that make me?"[54]

· · · · · · · · · · · · · · · ·

53. **oneiromancy** /ō'nīrə‚man(t)sē/ (n.) from the Greek *oneiros*, dream, and *manteia*, prophecy; the interpretation of dreams in order to foretell the future.

54. This is a question I have not been able to answer, mostly because it is my experience that Beatrice Orleans is undefinable; best I am able, they are a Proginoskes in human form. See also: *A Wind in the Door*, M. L'Engle.

THE ONE WHEREIN URSA ABERNATHY
CLIMBED A CLIFF

THE BEAR & BIRD | 48° 3′ 6″ NORTH & 90° 30′ 18″ WEST

[excerpts, interview with Beatrice Orleans]

We met under the boughs of a black pine, needles and cones raining down around us in a storm that came hard and fast off the lake.

It was early October in 1981, what my grandad would've called *a moosey day*. A mist you couldn't quite hold, low clouds, damp and humid-cold. Everything black and coral and yellow.

I was out in the late blueberries, eating more than I gathered, I'll admit. I saw Ursa first, as she was hopping and scraping and disappearing in and out of the basalt flows along the Granite River like a mink. At some point I watched as she scaled a sheer rock face bare-handed and I told myself, *Well, that's an apple I'd like to eat,* so I called out to her. *Hey-oh,* I yelled. *How's the view from the clouds up there?* She stared down at me and didn't say much for a minute. Then: *Better if you were up here with me!* She disappeared over the precipice.

I'm strong, but gravity is fond of my bones—meaning I do not climb. Trees or rocks or rope ladders. Hell, I hate climbing stairs some days ... but your grandma was worth trying for. I got about twelve feet off the ground before I froze in place, one foot on a crumbling chunk of granite, the other dangling in the wind, both hands clinging to the roots of a birch in the cliff face that was—slowly but obviously—loosening itself from the rock because of my weight. *A little help, darlin'?* I hollered up into the empty sky, not expecting to hear her laughing from below. I looked down, and there she was. *Now there's a better view,* she said. *Honey, lean out and let go.* Bless her, she'd come down to meet me. So I listened, and fell backward in a most ungraceful manner.

After she'd brushed the dirt off my ass and stanched my bleeding palms with mosses, she suggested we swim in the Inland Sea. We found a cove with a series of pools and caverns, stripped off our clothes on the rocks, and jumped in—quick, without looking. The lake was icy but warmer than the air. Wind making whitecapped ten-footers. We shrieked and whooped. I said something cheesy, how I'd *never felt so much like lightning*. Very rom-com. She was a better swimmer. I remember struggling to keep my eyes above the waves, following the sleek of her neck, the bright plum of her lips in the cold.

I had long been self-conscious of the roundness of my belly, the ripples of fat across my ribs and spine, but I noticed she kept blushing whenever I caught her watching, so I swam to a shallow spot and stood up, all but my ankles exposed. She had her back to me; before I could stop myself I called out to her again: *Hey-oh—how's the view from the lake?* I'll never forget the way she turned around.

She tread in the waves and looked on and I was terrified that she would stay there so long I'd lose my nerve and slip back under the surface, or that she would turn around again and disappear into the waves, that she would drift parallel down the shoreline until she had gotten just clear enough to escape. Somehow, I stood still and let her see. When she finally moved, she swam straight toward the shore. She came out of the water flushed, murmuring. I bent but she said, *No, stay just as you are* and her hands climbed my calves, the slope of my lower back.

Good lord, she said. *How gorgeous, my god.*

THE PAPER MOON MENAGERIE
The Hole in the Inland Sea
108 O... Shore Road, Beau Caelais

SUBMISSION FORM

NAME: TE: SERIAL NUMBER: 103567

LOCATION OF DISCOV... OURCE:

...EM DESCRIPTI...

To reco... ...bal description: pick up the hand-set and place ...rmly beside your ear ...nd mouth. Wait for the sound of the Inland Sea to peak in roaring before you dial. The number is irrelevant, although it must contain at least 10 digits, and we have noticed less static in records left for local area codes and 1-800 numbers ending in puns. Speak clearly into the hand-set, but do not shout. Use your native language. Singing is permitted so long as the singer is mostly in tune. Video translation for sign language speakers available by request.

Specimen collection: if there are no c... ...in size or material, please consult with management. **Do not** ...ance, abandon, loose, release, upend, or purposefully forge...

In the case that you either do not p... ...e exist any longer a physical remnant - whole or in part ...), please do utilize one of the provided **Containers for the** ...e empty container in the collection microcosm. Record and ...ate serial number on any and all forms of record, and ...your specimen(s) as specifically as possible.

▲ FIGURE 25.16 **Black-Hole Masses** Careful observations of nearby normal and active galaxies reveal that the mass of the central black hole is well correlated with the mass of the galactic bulge. In this diagram, each point represents a different galaxy. The straight line is the best fit to the data, implying a black-hole mass of 1/200 the mass of the bulge. (Data courtesy L. Ferrarese)

PATRICK BAILEY SINGS THE BLUES SO WELL

HOME | 48° 12' 57" NORTH & 90° 55' 23" WEST

3 December 2016

After I found the Paper Moon Menagerie on the beach, I dragged the trunk toward the cabin and covered it in pine shrug and snow. I crept back inside, lay down by the fire, and slept fitfully. Woke up again and again and again. Gave up, finally, just before dawn. I could hear Dad on the dock with his resonator—he played sometimes to keep himself awake between double shifts on the Water Shuttle, but never so late into the winter. I came outside wrapped in blankets, which still did not stop the wind from biting.

He paused picking.

"Hey kiddo," he said. "Can't sleep?"

"Dad," I said. "It's cold. Can you even feel your fingers?"

"Can't feel much," he said. "C'mon, sit by me a minute. It's gonna be warm today."

It wasn't. The snow had slowed and the wind was low, but it was still well below freezing. He was usually a fast picker, sharp and playful, but I could tell he was intentionally playing round and slow.

"What'd'ya wanna hear?" he asked.

"Some of Ma's songs," I said. "Old stuff. 'I Dreamed I Saw Big Blue Last Night.'"

Dad started tapping his big work boot against the dock for the drum.

"Nah, honey," he said, and stopped. "Grab my harmonica out of the case and play along."

First his boot, and then the jangle of his strings. Then he paused them both, leaned back and let out.

Ain't no grave

Ain't no grave, gonna hold my body down—[55]

. . . .

55. I love this song. Even as a child, I was drawn to melancholy, though if I'd known its

The Inland Sea made echoes of him, an invisible choir perpetually rolling toward us. His voice rang, cracked, rose. He tilted his head sideways toward the moon, eyes shut, mouth a tight-grin grimace. When he wound down to begin the first verse, he took one deep, ragged breath.

Patrick Bailey sings the blues so well, my mother often liked to say, *even the loons sit back and listen.*

When he started up again, I could feel the fight rise off him.[56]

. . . .

origins—a song about consumption, the disease that drowns from the inside out—it might have been too sharp, too painful a reminder.

56. In the time between my mother's disappearance and the compilation of these interviews, this was the first and only time I saw him cry. Dad is not the kind of man who holds back tears—in fact, I would say he likely cries more than my mother, myself, and Aunt Bea combined, especially now that I'm older and he's become *a sentimental old bastard,* as he likes to say. But I imagine this, during the most uneasy Time of Missing, was the kind of hurt that he knew he'd not be able to end if he started. Part of him needed to howl, another to bury it down. The only way he knew to process was to play.

SHE'D NOT YET SHORN HER HAIR TO THE SCALP

THE BEAR & BIRD | 48° 3' 6" NORTH & 90° 30' 18" WEST

[excerpts, interview with Beatrice Orleans]

It was simple. She put out the call on the shortwave, half-past nine in the morning, a Sunday.

Now seeking specimens for the Paper Moon Menagerie.

She flyer'd the county with instructions, mailed out packages with request envelopes to the Big City and beyond.

At first, it was just the old shipping container she *liberated* from a Mesabi junkyard with the help of some of my other Sunday House kids and an abandoned tractor-trailer,[57] but she added an astrolabe, a greenhouse, and that steamer trunk she left you. Final touch was a mildewed lighthouse that never did shine; four feet by nine, made of Plexiglas and iron. *LOCAL CALLS ONLY* she'd stenciled in black letters above the accordion door.

Folks mostly drove, given how far we were from everything but the Inland Sea, until the fuel shortages started—then they showed up on bicycles, by horse, in worn boots, barefoot, bleeding. Sometimes one or two in a day, sometimes a steady line like congregants down to the river. They came with children and animals in tow, sacks of belongings on their backs. Dusty, dirty, tired but finally arrived and therefore unburdened, at least partially. Folks leaned on each other. They waited. If they'd been wealthy before, in folding chairs, three-season tents; most slept curled on sidewalks, on quilts

....

57. Police reports indicate a theft was reported at the Ruin Lake Branch yard in the spring of 1999, including: 8' × 8' × 20' shipping container, three gallons of industrial-grade black paint, and a number of hand tools. No charges were ever filed.

and beach towels, wrapped in garbage bags against the cold, the rain, and the wind off the water.

Once word started to spread, they showed up more and more frequently. Nobody spoke except to share where they'd come from, what they'd brought that needed saving. Rumors they'd heard about her and the witchy shit she was accomplishing. Of this, they could not stop talking.

> *Is it true she can turn herself into a bird?*
> *My neighbor says her hands and feet are webbed.*

Oh honey, I wish you could've seen her—all those people, come from so. very. far. They'd murmur, gasp, *oooh*, and wolf-whistle when she stepped out.
And tell me, she'd say, *where's home for you?*
I can see her: clasped palms and touched cheeks, babies held aloft to kiss.
So good to see you here, sir. So good.
A pagan tent-revival preacher on the night before the Rapture.

Folks gave her their specimens, then pressed small gifts into her hands in gratitude—ribbon, speckled stones, home-baked goods, tinctures, bouquets of thistle and lace. She drifted between them; she spoke and they answered. *How strong you must be. Bless you, ma'am, for making the journey.*

No matter how ugly or small or common, she'd stop to inspect whatever they brought her. Jars of insects or fish, seeds.[58] Cages of flapping birds. Literal pieces of their homes—potted sections of prairie and pine forest and oak savanna, shoeboxes full of silt. Sometimes it'd been too late, and in lieu of things too fragile or too lost to bring, folks gave her tiny dioramas and

----

58. See also: *Examples of Microcosm Deposits*, pp. TK.

pencil sketches, paper sculptures that they'd made and carried, of glaciers and river basins and the bottoms of the oceans. She loved those especially.

Such a beauty.

The last one?

Ours is important work.

I saw what it meant when she smiled at them, shared their frustration, mirrored their sorrow. When she put a hand at their back or furrowed her brow. Felt their particular loss. Then she'd climb into her Moon Booth and point to the sky. *Now is the time we remember together.* The crowd would go dead quiet, step forward one at a time, and stand before her, hold out their hands.

You know—she was barely five feet tall, but everyone knew when she appeared. Your mother was a sparkler in a field after dusk. And in those days she was stunning: she'd not yet shorn her hair to the scalp; not yet stopped bathing. Thick and strong like that black pine on Little Ghost used to be before it got rot and leaned over on its roots in your yard.

At the time, it was difficult to walk in the woods near Ruin Lake without stepping on an anonymous offering. Makes me wonder now, when I'm walking around Beau Caelais: which of these people who pretend you do not exist, who pretend that she no longer exists either—which among them

might've left something for her out in your woods, hoping. Before.

The Beau Caelais Daily

VOL. I...No. 1   Caelais County News for the North Country   YESTERDAY'S NEWS TODAY   www.beaucaelaistoday.com   *NIGHT EDITION*

812 DEAD BIRDS FOUND

TOXIC SLURRY AT MESABI SITE BLAMED

Ecologists Concerned for Species Survival

ELSA BIRCH · BEAU CAELAIS

. . . .

59. See also: Map. According to her journals, my mother buried all but one of the birds
from the *Paper Moon Menagerie* near the intersection of Ruin and Church, before
she brought them Below. At that intersection burial ground today, you might find
a few pintails or a crushed bit of guano, but she would later unbury them, their
snapped wings and missing beaks and tiny broken feet having been resurrected. It
was a shallow grave and a mess of feathers, five hundred yards up the burnt slope
from where the Caelais County Aquatic Patrol found Hugo Mitchum in Ruin. She
kept the loon for herself, as well as its mate. Sixteen years later, it was the same male
who escaped through the star-loft glass, and the female who came back to me, bloodied and trapped in that blue globe.

EVIDENCE

- snow eagle
- pine tar pepper tit
- limestone swift
- a three-winged raven
- two pairs of blue sun owls
- an oil slick honeycreeper
- a clutch of purple-legged king crown ice ibis,
  still in their shells
  —excerpt, bird spp. committed to the Paper Moon Menagerie

I showed up with a bucket of dust bowl and the body of my gran's last rosebud quail. Carried it from my family's homestead—first in the bed of my flatbed pickup, and when that broke down just south of lake country, on foot. Eight hundred miles to this place I'd heard about on the radio called *Beau Caelais*. I almost stopped a dozen times, but I just kept hearing that voice: *Now seeking specimens to be saved.* When I stepped up to your mother, she took my dirt gently, and asked me what it meant, where I'd come from. *This is what's left of our bit of the Aquifer,* I told her. *We learned to live on next to nothing, but we didn't realize how much more nothing nothing could become.* She said a few words while she let the dust settle in a simple paper bag. Took the bird from me and cradled it in her hands like Gran used to. *So soft*, she said, and put it in a glass box with its head nestled on its wings. We reminisced on homemade piecrusts, the reward of sore shoulders and sunburn. I remember when I turned and started back—eight hundred miles to a home that no longer existed—I was no longer pulsing with hurt. I don't use that word lightly, *pulsing*. I used to feel that heartache fucking pump through my lungs, in my skin. She lifted it all away. I don't think it had shit to do with saving a handful of land, putting a bird in a box, and carrying it down into a magic hole.

—Molly Schwert Bear, seventh-generation farmer, contributor no. 387

And the Lord doth sayeth: Women, mine own most powerful in the World of Men. No, a' course. That isn't in there, ya know. I just like to say it every now and again, remind myself.

—The Rev. Jack Olafssen, Saint Ernestine's Lutheran Mission,
Beau Caelais

drown / droun / (v.) from the Old Norse *drukkna,* Old English *drucnian* or *drounen,* meaning to suffocate by immersion in water; to overwhelm by rising above as a flood; to be swallowed up by water (originally of ships as well as living things); likely re *drincan,* to drink. See also: head low in the water, mouth open, eyes glassy and empty, fear evident; hyperventilating, gasping; trying and failing to swim; inhalation; deluge; inundate, as in a flood.

Tattoo my name on the back of your tongue | Speak loud my name till I wake from the lake.

—Hymn no. 13, Beau Caelais, Trad. Spiritual

THE PAPER MOON MENAGERIE
The Hole in the Inland Sea
108 Old Shore Road, Beau Caelais

SUBMISSION FORM

NAME: DATE: SERIAL NUMBER: 256Ø

LOCATION OF DISCOVERY/SOURCE:

ITEM DESCRIPTION:

To record verbal [...]ck up the hand-set and place [...]
your ear and mouth. Wait [...] the sound of the Inland Sea [...]eak[...]
before you dial. The number is irrelevant, although it must [...]ain at [...]
digits, and we have noticed less static in records left [...] local area[...]
and 1-800 numbers ending in puns. Speak clearly into the hand-set, but do [...]
shout. Use your native langua[...]. Singing is permitted so long as the singer [...]
mostly in tune. Video translation for sign language speakers available [...]
request.

Sp[...]m[...] collection: if there are no containers appropriate in size or material,
pl[...]e [...]nsult with management. **Do not**, under any circumstance, abandon, loose,
re[...]se, [...]end, or purposefully forget your specimen.

In th[...] [...] that you either do not possess nor does there exist any longer a
ph[...] [...]nt - whole or in part - of your specimen(s), please do utilize
[...] rovided **Containers for the Too Late**. Deposit the empty container in
[...]en microcosm. Record and indicate the appropriate serial number on
[...]ll forms of record, and take care to detail your specimen(s) as
[...]lly as possible.

THE DEVIL LIVES IN THE WILD RICE ON RUIN

RUIN LAKE | 48° 12' 09" NORTH & 90° 52' 29" WEST

5 December 2016

Dad radioed Aunt Bea to say he would be in the North Country until the next morning, so they called me over our shortwave and asked me to hurry to the bar before sundown.

"I won't leave you out on the island alone," they said. "But you're not to drink anything stronger than sparkling cider. No bullshit, girl."

I knew my mother wouldn't be anywhere near town. Still, I checked for her at all the places in Beau Caelais she used to pass her time protesting: at the QuikMart grocery, the abandoned gas station, the portico outside the bank where the houseless folx she brewed moonshine for liked to sleep. The public library was closed, or I would have gone inside, at least to escape the cold for a moment. As the sun went, unease settled in me and I thought about running home or yelling out her name, sitting down on the side of the road to wait, pathetic and passive. Then I turned toward the bar, two miles out into the North Country on a road above the remains of Ruin Lake.

The storm had left drifts of ash-dirty snow muraled along the road that led between Beau Caelais and the Mesabi site, and soon there were no prints but mine.[60] My toes froze in my boots. Rips of ice caught in my socks

. . . .

60. The stretch that runs from the Inland Sea through town and into the woods used to hum with copper miners, iron miners, timber trucks, tourists in the summer season. By that winter, it was a crumbling vein of asphalt and sphagnum. All I had ever known of the isthmus lowlands east of town was a dead zone of blackened trees, a place that smelled perpetually of burning. The North Woods were really no longer there, though everyone still referred to them as if they were. Ruin Lake has grown into its name—it had taken tens of thousands of years and the slow, weighty wearing of the glaciers to leave an impression eighty-three feet deep and just more than nine hundred feet long in a plate of granite and iron; it took a few moments, a spark in the

and against my shins. I held my breath; listened for snapping branches; kept my head down for the wind, for fear of what I might see. The incessant sound of the Inland Sea pressing against the shore grew faint as I walked east, south. Pines showed their lost needles in reddish chunks and dropped branches, stark dead posts. An abandoned sign pointed me in the right direction, though soon I could smell it. Sulfur, iron, sour, rot. *Mesabi Mine Co., Ruin Lake Branch.*

In the darkening sky a kettle of grackles, fisher ravens, and pine crows flew in circles. My mother used to say that birds boiled right before they were going to leave for somewhere far away.

Imminent escape, she'd say, and point. *Hold your breath and watch them go.*

Below the kettle, hundreds floundered on the slurry of the lake. The surface of Ruin was covered in a layer of snow, but the ice was thin and birds had fallen through. Some had gone drunk and loopy. They'd try to fly and spasm instead, spiral, run into each other sideways and upside down, dive and crash. I watched as they sank and squawked, and with each flap, mired farther, wings splayed like powder burns.

Out in the woods, the bar was the only business still open, its two-story frame leaning low over the hill above Ruin. A neon sign blinked blue *BE R* in the distance, and as I grew nearer I felt as if I was being followed. Crunching ice, a wheeze. I turned and saw nothing. Bears were rare, and shy. Wolves long gone after the moose. *A stray dog maybe, or a raccoon, a rat.* Every sound around me amplified. A branch snapped, and I stopped still in the middle of the road. Listened harder, and thought I heard the sound of singing, high sad harmonies. The wind. My mother echoed in my head—advice she had given to me, had been given, she used to say, by the Women   Beneath.

Keep your keys in your hand.

. . . .

wrong kind of wind, to turn it to a soup of algae and bones that freezes ice the color of oil.

Ears open. Eyes up. Wear sensible shoes.

Learn to dilate every nerve, every muscle cell in self-preservation.

Never move unaware of your tenuous place.

I wouldn't turn around, wouldn't look into the woods-that-were-not-woods.

Keep your eyes on the light.

I breathed in, and in again, but I was too curious. The dusk, the haze of ashes, the winter air glowing with its own cold—it all made shapes of nothing, obscured shapes in nothing, too.

"Hello?" I called. And then, as if I had summoned him, *stupid*, he was there in the fog.

I saw that white eye glowing in his too-thin skull first, then his hulking shoulders, his huge hands protruding from a sweater that did not fit, the thread-bare fabric smeared with what might have been mud, maybe blood, or feces, both. He raised one hand and pointed.

"You," he said, and pointed again. "Queen of dark birds."

For all my mother's warnings, I was still the sort of girl whose best defense was to diffuse any aggressor with kindness, the girl who had not yet learned it was necessary to be rude or loud or offensive for self-preservation. And so I asked him to repeat himself.

"Sorry?" I said. "I didn't—what did you say?"

I stepped forward even,[61] but this seemed to agitate him more. He lurched toward me.

"We made moon bones," he said, pointing at me with the elbow of his lame wing, his six-foot-something frame looming.

I don't remember what brought my mother's insistent voice into my head, the roaring of my blood, saying:

Run.

Run.

Run.

Adrenaline broke and I startled. The bar was hardly more than a quarter

....

61. Who does this? Every girl, at some point, I promise.

mile away, and as I reached for the door, a cold wind cut through me. Aunt Bea looked up when I came in; smiled, turned to pour a steaming mug of cider at the bar. I was sure some dark hand had just missed me. A man? A demon? *The Devil lives in the wild rice on Ruin.*

I bent, gasping.[62]

---

62. Breathe, cough. Breathe deeper, cough and cough and cough. Wheeze, whine, whistle. Cough, cough, fight for breath, blue, breathe, wheeze, whistle, cough. Cough. Spit and bend, heave. Heave. Wheeze and heave. Cough and gasp and swallow. Bear breathe, wheeze. Chuff, cough. Chuff. Chuff. Chuff. Bend and heave. Blue. Breathe. Blue. Breathe. Heave, heave. Gasp and gasp for breath. Fight blue, burst, swallow air and cough again. Hitch swallow halt and falter. Cough. Cough. Whistle. Fill and thistle, hitch, catch, hack cough panic breath gasp and cough and bend and heave. Reeve. Shallow, swallow, shallow, swallow. Wheeze wheeze wheeze. Breathe in and in and in. Breathe breathe breathe. Hitch and catch. Falter, wheeze. The water ebbs and rises. The water flows and falters. Cough, hitch, bubble, blue. Wheeze, whine. Whine, whistle. Breathe in and in and in.

You sure nobody's gonna hear this except the judge? I don't want anybody to hear this. Can Ms. Orleans stay in here with me? She said she can stay.[64]

Where do you want me to start?—Okay.

Yeah, at Mesabi. My first day he told me I looked good in the uniform. *I'mma need a new pair of pants, you keep fillin' yours out like that, boy.* We were on line in the North Country, one of the sulfur wells.

Twenty, twenty-five men. I think I was younger than—I was the youngest by about three years. The kid.

I know how big I am. I hate it. All I want is to be invisible, most days. But it's all anybody ever says. *You part tree, boy? You part moose?*

So Hugo hits on me, some of the others laugh, we all go back to digging. Thought he was making fun of me.

All I ever hear is *Buck the fuck up,* or *Why you always gotta be such a girl,* or *You're such a fuckin' faerie, Ellis.*

Yeah, I mean he winked at me and grabbed my ass. I blushed and everybody saw. Thought he was making fun.

....

63. See also: pp. TK.
64. §895.45(1)(c) complainants of certain abusive or violent crimes are entitled to request an advocate, who may provide emotional support and accompaniment to court hearings, witness proceedings, and legal interviews such as police investigations, medical exams, and discovery depositions.

Why? I mean, that's a hard question—

No, I'm not trying to be difficult. I don't understand what you want me to say.

What does that have to do with what happened to—Okay fine. No, I'm fine.

Uh, yeah. Since I was about six. I'm the effeminate Olsen, even compared to my sisters. Can't shoot a gun to save my life. Never had many friends—my brothers made sure everybody knew I was—anyway.

No, he's not attractive. He's an asshole. Everybody knows he's an asshole.

It's like I was starving, and he gave me a bloody flank steak on a plate.[65] You never felt that way?

· · · · · · · · · · · · · · · · · ·

65. In my interviews, folks always say things like *Don't get what Ellis saw in Hugo. Ellis was such a nice boy* . . . or *If there ever was an odd pair* . . . Hugo is described as quick to argue over useless or trivial things like darts, bar tabs, the upcoming weather. Ellis, almost entirely the opposite—deliberate, a plainspoken, second-generation Swede, the quiet giant of his family who kept to himself, and seemed to prefer to pass his increasing spare time away from work by catching and frying his own walleye. When hours on the Ruin Lake excavation site got cut, Hugo and Ellis would have been in danger of losing their jobs, being lower on the seniority list for assignments, even with serious familial connections in the company.

I AM DREAMING OF THE WOMEN   BENEATH

[excerpt, *The Collected Journals of Marietta Abernathy*]

22 JUNE 1999[66]

I drowned   after he was done with me.

Facedown in the murk and gloom, I caught sight of my mother: the one they called Ursa, a woman I'd never met until now.
We were both of us blue.
           Beneath.
Her on account of the bleeding out,   me just cut from her body.
    Me on account of that fucker   Hugo Mitchum,
on account of the Solstice moon, how I swallowed all that water. How I saw through to this place Between, how I'm waiting on this Other Side.
Ursa met me there.
"Welcome, dear, but you're early," she said, bubbles blooming from her lips. "You can stay the night. It's a long trip back. I can't let you set down and sit here just yet. You've got work to do up there, Above."
She reached her long, strong hands toward the surface and pulled me under, down down down into the Hole below. At the mouth, she let go and paused. Her hair spread in a halo. She beckoned, went through. I followed.

At first I thought we'd traveled nowhere other than back up out of the water and into the outskirts of Beau Caelais, to the wide, unending shore.

. . . .

66. At this time, Marietta Abernathy, emancipated minor, approximately sixteen years of age.

It seemed identical, until I realized it was an inverse of Above, a mirror with eerie glitches:

Birches were black with white paper knots.
Ravens flew from right to left, belly-up.
Pinpricks of light in the clouded-over sky showed through—not to stars, but to the water of a lake caught behind some invisible barrier, as if a giant glass case surrounded this place where Ursa had brought me.

I looked around and noticed we were not alone. There were Women Beneath everywhere, in various states of undress and putrefaction. Dead but not quite, all of them absentmindedly existing in the After. They plucked at the rips in their skin, and at the ruby-blue berries growing healthy all around. They yanked loose teeth from their mouths, winced at the yellowing bruises painted across their ribs, then went back to scrubbing their socks in the water, breastfeeding their babies. They ran their fingers through clumps of hair and pulled away pieces of scalp, laughing and chatting. So many were nearly naked; their shirts in rags, pants missing, one tit hanging out or bare-assed and -vulva'd, but they seemed unbothered, shameless.
Then
some un   expected gunshot crack in the underbrush sent them startling like swallows,
and for a moment the World Below buzzed

a high-pitched heat   whine of cicaaaaaaadas.

These Women   Beneath,
   their eyes shone white in their skulls
   they darted,
   crooned,
   dug holes in the ground and covered their wounds with soil,

                                    pine boughs.
One of them hollering:
               bludgeoned the seat of her fiberglass kayak with a
               skillet over and over and over.
Another spit and
           rattled like a snake caught in a trap   .

FIGHT,   f l i g h t,   or   freeze.

Soon, though,   they settled.
One of them started to hum, and then to sing a   single held sound.[67]
It carried from her
                to the next,   until
                        each of them found a
                        space in the harmony.
                Like a chorus of harmoniums,
                Gregorian monks,   they sang;   ruffled
                    their limbs;
                chanted;   shook their hair; rippled
                   in their skins.

The Leader of the Humming stopped, and held her hands out at her sides,
   palms up.
They all stopped. They all breathed in,   and in, and

                                  in

. . . .

67. See also: p. TK.

and in unison, they breathed out.

                                Black flies poured from their mouths.

The flies shimmered and floated in the air around us and then dissipated
   upward, into Above.
The Women   Beneath returned to their just-above-baseline
   stasis of function.

Some I recognized from rumor, newspaper articles.[68]
A few I'd seen in life, around town—

the One Whose Head Had Been Cracked Open Like a Melon[69]
the One Who Was Left Sprawled in the Ditch Down Highway 61[70]
the Six-Year-Old Twins Who Were Stolen[71]
the Blinded Wife[72]
the One with a Necklace of Handprints[73]

. . . .

68. VAWnet reports that women are more likely to be killed by an intimate partner (husband, boyfriend, [same-sex] partner, or ex) than by anyone else (*Catalano, 2013; Violence Policy Center, 2015*). Approximately 2 out of 5 female murder victims are killed by an intimate partner (*Cooper & Smith, 2011*). In 2013, fifteen times as many females were murdered by a male they knew than were killed by male strangers. For victims who knew their offenders, 62% were wives, common-law wives, ex-wives, or girlfriends of the offenders (*Violence Policy Center, 2015*). Roughly one in three women will experience physical violence by a partner in their lifetime. Black women are two and a half times more likely to be killed than white women. According to the 2015 U.S. Transgender Survey, nearly half of respondents had been sexually assaulted in their lifetimes; even more had experienced domestic violence. As many as 84% of Native women report experiencing violence, of whom as many as 97% report being harmed by non-Native men. There have been 2,448 reported cases of Missing and Murdered Indigenous Women, Girls, and Two Spirit since 1990; Indigenous relatives know there are many thousands more (*Sovereign Bodies Institute*). In the United States, it was officially confirmed that 1,218 women were killed by an intimate partner in 1999; 1,527 in 2017. Worldwide in 2020, one woman or girl was killed by a family member every eleven minutes.

69. Mariposa Walking Bear, 1934–1989. See also: pp. TK.

70. Jax Doe. If you know them or their loved ones, contact Det. Virginia Welch, Caelais Co. Sheriff Dept. with any pertinent information.

71. Raina and Ariette Valois, 1993–1999.

72. Berta Taylor, 1970–1994. Found disfigured and unconscious in her kitchen by her next-door neighbor; would later die of septic shock in the Caelais Co. emergency room. Though he maintains his innocence, her husband was convicted of simple mayhem and second-degree manslaughter for throwing cooking oil on her face. He would serve five years of a seven-year sentence, one year less than their marriage.

73. According to Dr. J. C. Campbell, +/- 50% of victims of intimate partner violence report having been strangled by their abusive partner. Though previous strangulation attempts are a common predicator of intimate partner homicide, few victims report such violence to law enforcement or medical professionals for fear they will not be

I looked and looked but never saw an end to them, this humming village, all these Women   Beneath sprawled along the upside-down rocky bottom. I vomited

heaving up Ruin, and Hugo.

A puddle the color of milk.

"What world is this? Why didn't I know?" I asked.

Ursa ignored me.

"You'll notice we're building," she said instead, gesturing around us. "The World As It Was is no longer sustainable. But someday, this one, the World Below could be. This is where you come in."

"How long have you been here? How many of you are there?" I asked.

"Bring everything you can manage," she said. "It's easiest to cross when the Boundary is calmed by ice, or on cool days in summer, when the wind is low, the moon full or new, and the water flat and smooth. But the Hole stays open as long as there are things Above that need keeping safe—"[74]

"Bring things?" I asked. "What things?"

I was so confused, a new

fear and an odd, comforting

anger starting to seep

into the ragged cuts that crisscrossed   my belly,

my palms,

the fluttering wheeze

. . . .

taken seriously, that their partners will be harmed or killed by police, or that they themselves will be incarcerated.

74. Having once acted the wise auntie to Persephone during the Time of Her Upsetting Imprisonment, you could think Hecate a bit of a doula between Above and Below. On ancient ceramic pots, she is depicted with three faces peering in ambivalence at a crossroads. Stories say she waits there for women to gather, whereafter it would be her duty to lead them all on the descent into Hades en masse. Though never confirmed, I like to imagine it was also Hecate who gave Lysistrata the sly idea for pacific sexual abstinence. At the very least they were co-conspirators.

of water　　　　making itself at home
in my lungs.

"Marietta, my dear girl," Ursa said. "You've already been collecting the Disappearing up there—"

"—your project!" said the Six-Year-Old Twins Who Were Stolen.

"What's it called?" said the Blinded Wife. "The Menagerie of the Moon? I like that. I miss its light."

"No, that's not right," said the One Who Was Left Sprawled in the Ditch Down Highway 61. "But whatever. Keep at it, except bring everything down here, where it's needed. All the good stuff. Whiskey, venison, bouquets of fireweed and bitter-berry. Fresh honey. Can you bring me some fresh honey? They don't deserve it up there. They don't deserve the bees. Bring the bees down here, too."

"They don't deserve *you*," said the One with a Necklace of Handprints.

"They don't deserve what you're doing," said the One Whose Head Had Been Cracked Open Like a Melon. "Take it from those who know."

"I don't understand what you're asking of me," I said, starting to cry.

Ursa put one hand to my cheek, caught the tears already falling. "I'm sorry this happened to you," she said. "You did nothing wrong."

"We're so, so sorry," they said in unison.

The rest of that night, the Women　　　　Beneath loved on me
fed me sweet bits of fish flesh and scraps
of blueberry pie hugged me
poured several ounces of juniper gin into
my mouth

but when I was feeling fat and happy,
when I had near forgotten the bruises blooming on my bloodied thighs,

Ursa told me I had to return to the World As It Was, Above.

"I can't go back and forth," she said. "It's—too much, the trip—but you can."
"Go back?" I asked.

I wanted nothing less. There was a poison growing roots, a cold spill pulling
my skin in tight. Hate.

"What do I do with this?" I said, and showed it to them.
They showed me theirs. Told me I would learn to manage it in time.
"It'll come to you," Ursa said. "You have work to do yet, darling."

When I came up gasping on the other side, I was there where they'd left
me. Draped in lily-weeds, smeared in mud. Hugo was gone, Ellis was gone,
the Solstice moon gone.

I was gone, too:
but I knew something new was there, inside. A girl I hadn't asked for.[75]

· · · · · · · · · · · · · · · · · · ·

75. Patrick Bailey is not my father, but this has not ever mattered to either of us. He as
much as told me when I was small, five or six. She was Missing, and he was afraid.
He said, *You're not mine but I'll never leave you behind.* I realized, much later, what
it was he was afraid of: that they'd take me away from him if she never came back.
That they'd give me to the Other. My mother first describes Dad in her journal as *a
man with rough hands, cheeks and hair sun-bleached from the brightness of the North
Country. Lena took to him straightaway,* she writes. *So I figure.* Dad explains it a little
differently. *What can I say? Mar found me, brought me home.* He says she had a way
of making *home* of people. She was a builder of worlds—things solid, fluid, both or
neither. But he was the one who taught me to sing. Most often it was him who tucked
me in, hemmed my secondhand jeans, called me honeybun. What does it mean to
belong to each other? *You're mine.* It is communal, adoring; it is possessive and stran-
gling. Eventually, I became Emalene Bailey, but I will always be an Abernathy, girl of
the North Country and the Women   Beneath.

HOW DO WE LOVE ON EACH OTHER? HOW DO WE HOLD ON TO OURSELVES?[76]

HOME | 48° 12′ 57″ NORTH & 90° 55′ 23″ WEST

Sex, or even general physical intimacy—
    who has it with whom;
    for whom it is pleasurable, and how;
    how to express it;
    how to consent to it, speak about it, ask for it or deny it;
    how to take care of ourselves—
these were not things that we discussed on Little Ghost.

In retrospect: at best, my mother had always seemed uninterested, and Dad often just seemed tired. The Water Shuttle kept him sometimes twenty hours a day. She complained of unexplainable pains in her shoulders. He moved around her as if she were like her specimens. She hugged him, but not really. All physical contact she had with us was limited, as if she were infectious.

More than once, I woke up thirsty in the middle of the night to find her curled in her canoe in the yard. Sometimes she even looked at me as if she were surprised by my face, as if

        I had snuck up on her in the dark.

. . . .

76. A question Aunt Bea asks me often. See also: p. TK.

EVIDENCE

Listen, girl. She made trouble for everybody, herself included. So did your grandma. My job is to take care of the folks in this county, uphold the law. Keep the peace. I respond when I see something needs responding to. You gonna make trouble, too?

—Sheriff Gregor Shultze, Caelais Co. 1989–present

Seventeen years, my boy marked for somethin' ain't never been proved. Now he's dead. Not his fault y'all are crazy.

—Rita Mae Mitchum, teacher at Beau Caelais Elementary School, mother of Hugo

We surround you, listening, watching. We move through the earth beneath you, osmosing time as it leaks and spreads itself thin. Where there is empty space, we fill. Our beds are in the spidered veins of shale and granite and sandstone, the curved echoes of primordial ice that we remember in our ancient weight. When we need to go where there is no way, we leave our own bodies behind and borrow the bones of the others to travel, to reach you, to find and take what we need. Our eyes reflect the old world in new ways, the light of the other worlds below. Pass through us, divide us, define others by us. We rise and fall according to no man. The Insomnia of Ashes was the only way she knew to make you listen.   —The Boundary Waters

Tears in the space-time continuum insist the divisions we draw are narrow-minded, ephemeral. *This is part of that. What happens here eventually seeps into there.* It's just that we're tiny, short-lived monkeys who imagine ourselves into the center of everything. Spatial relational directional locative narrative labeling, it's all ego, man. Sooner we learn that, the better off we'll all be. Sign me up for a trip through the atomizer! Sounds fun, sure. But we don't always need intricate, million-dollar machines to speak across the divide. What the hell else is a photograph, words set down?

—Prof. Louise Okpik Bass, co-chair, Relativistic Physics & Wormhole
Mechanics, College of the North Woods

Fucking flies up here. Black, tiny, biting. Scourge of the North Woods.
Only got worse after what happened to your mother. *A plague on both your houses.*

—Frank Delacroix, Caelais Co. Aquatic Patrol, retired site chief, Mesabi
Mine Co., Ruin Lake Branch

Call me banshee, beggar, bitch. I fight for the breath. I fight for the others.
I fight for the ones that cannot shriek and wail in your face because you've
muzzled them. Call me banshee, I don't give a shit. Mine is a holy fight.

—Ursa Abernathy, the Mountain Who Stood Against the Mine, quoted
in the *Beau Caelais Daily* three days before her death

ELLIS WAS QUIET, A LITTLE QUEER

CAELAIS CO. WILDERNESS SERVICE, RUIN LAKE STATION | 48° 4' 15" NORTH & 90° 39' 19" WEST

[excerpts, interview with Deputy Ranger Ingrid Solberg-Black]

There's lots a' Swedes up here, but Ellis's family is hard to miss. Tall motherfuckers, all of 'em, even the women. Broad and slow, like bears just woke in winter. Blonder than blond. Pale eyes. Run into one in the dark, you'd swear they'd see straight through you. Doesn't make 'em less intimidating that Ole Ironsen is one of the richest timber barons in the history of the North Country.

Ellis's older brothers are all kinda rowdy, known to be rough on their women, but he was quiet, a little queer.

According to Frank, the Mitchum kid was the one on the schedule, but it was Ellis Olsen on watch at Ruin that night. Folks say Hugo used to bully Ellis into taking his shifts. You wouldn't think it'd work that way to look at them—Hugo was about five foot eight, maybe a hundred fifty pounds on a day when he'd had steak for breakfast, and Ellis is six four easy, big as a moose even after what happened. But Hugo's older than Ellis by three or four years, and you could tell the kid looked up to him. When the rescue crew found Ellis three days after the flames went down, they brought him to the ER, called me to sit with him in the burn unit.

NOW, THIS WAS YOUR MOTHER BEFORE MITCHUM

NOT BEFORE YOU.

THERE'S A DIFFERENCE, AND I NEED YOU TO
REMEMBER THAT.

Aunt Bea

DON'T MAKE A SCENE

8 December 2016

My mother homeschooled me until I was nine and a half, until her Times of Missing really picked up steam and keeping me home was no longer tenable. Dad couldn't stay with me or we'd have nothing to eat, and so they decided I should attend the tiny mixed-grade school in the Caelais Co. Public Library basement on the mainland.[77] In a town of less than three hundred, in a school of twenty-seven,[78] approximately twenty-six did not speak to me because I was *that Abernathy's daughter.*

I remember my first day as one of acute alienation, the oblivious cruelty of children who smelled weakness, and I went to my mother for sympathy that afternoon when I'd walked back home across the land bridge to Little Ghost, alone.

"No one would play duck duck gray duck with me," I said.

"Is that so," she responded, birch dust and pine resin frosting her hair.

While she stood in our kitchen over a giant paper press, preserving the fallen leaves, petals, and pollen from the most recent patch of North Country to have withered and grayed into the Collapse, she listened without eye contact.

"Ms. Mitchum said they didn't have to," I said. "It's not fair."

. . . .

77. See Map.

78. Population geneticists would likely recognize this to be a high ratio of adults to children, though these numbers are shifting closer to the mean. It appears the Insomnia of Ashes created the opposite of a reproductive boom, as there were very few infants born in Caelais Co. or the surrounding areas between late 1999 and 2002, and a slow increase thereafter. Research and anecdotal documentation suggests this may be in part due to psychological and spiritual despair, but it is also likely due to the harmful environmental consequences observed re mammalian gestation and birthing.

"Rita Mae Mitchum is a bitch," she said.

I'd never heard that word before.

"What's that mean, Ma," I asked.

"Never you mind," she said over her shoulder. "C'mere and hold this pine bough for me quick."

Onward, without looking up from her work.

Seven years later, during the winter of the Storm Wherein My Mother Vanished, Hugo Mitchum's mother was still the only teacher at that tiny school. In the days after Hugo was found, Rita Mae Mitchum sneered at me even more than before, drew big fat zeros in red pen on my assignments without bothering to read them—but she never spoke to me directly. That, she left to the boys in the school.

"Witch, bitch, pussy willow," they'd tease, hands reaching down my jeans.

According to them the Loon Woman was wild, her mouth loose. As were her legs. My mother—and by association, me—was a whore, a girl who needed told. A smart piece of ass who was always, evermore asking for it, but—

"Don't make a scene." They'd laugh when I told them to leave me alone. "What's the big deal?"

"You gonna stab me for lookin'?"

"No? You a lezzo or somethin', like your grandma?"

"Don't be a prude—"

I was the One Who Refused to be the correct kind of sexual, the One Who Rejected Her Own Objectification, and therefore it was me who made trouble, not the boys who drank cheap wine in the parking lot at lunch and then breathed down my neck during chemistry, who left their dicks hanging out intentionally after phys ed.

"What? Don't like what you see?"

I didn't tell Dad, wouldn't; I didn't want to burden him with more hurt, was mildly afraid of what he might do to the boys if I mentioned anything. Aunt Bea used to see it on me and intuitively ask if I was okay.

I'd say yes, but still: I thought maybe I deserved it; if then my mother was deserving also.

One day, Donald Hawthorne followed me into the textbook closet and tried to kiss me. I pushed him and he backed away, came back. He hollered when I grabbed at his crotch.

"What?" I said. "You thought I was asking?"

He pushed me back, two hands on my tits, and he left them there when he leaned into me, leering. He backed off, but I felt his fingers like a burn.

"Don't make a scene," he said.

I didn't, not really. I wanted to: I could have screamed obscenities; taken both hands and overturned my desk, his desk, all the furniture in the room. I could have ripped at the map of the Inland Sea pinned to the wall, picked up his books and thrown them at his head, taken the coffee cup off Rita Mae Mitchum's desk and thrown it against the ground. I could have pointed at him and made everyone pay me attention while I called him what he was. But I didn't do any of those things—instead, I walked to the doorway and took my coat very quietly off its hook. I reached for the door-knob without even making a sound. Still though, that wasn't good enough.

"Where you going, girl?" Rita Mae Mitchum said. "Class ain't finished yet."

I opened my mouth, paused.

"Not feeling well," I muttered.

"I didn't hear you," she said.

"I said I'm not feeling well." A little louder. "I'm going home."

"So you leave," she said, shaking her head. "Weak, just like—"

At this I snapped.

"Oh, fuck you," I said.

Immediately, all those boys started hooting—*ohhhh whaat?! You hear her?* Most of the girls in the class looked down or away, but some of the younger ones piped up in reinforcement. *Ms. Mitchum, she just—Ms. Mitchum, what are you going to do? Ms. Mitchum—*

Rita Mae Mitchum turned pink, from the top of her cornflower collar to the shiny patches on her balding head, but she didn't yell or threaten me or even stand up from her desk. She smirked.

"You're done here, Emalene," she said. "Don't come back tomorrow."

It was the middle of the day, and I was so angry I didn't know what to do with myself. I thought about going to see Aunt Bea at the bar. Of going out in my mother's sea kayak and paddling as far as my arms would carry me. I imagined cresting the horizon into the North Country, of dumping the boat, of wading into the lake and leaning into the waves and just breathing in. A part of me was angry at the Inland Sea, too, and the only way I could think to show it was to drink and drink and drink, until either I or it or both of us had disappeared. I tried to slow my breath down but I had already started to wheeze.[79]

----

79. What other evidence do I have of my own hydratic lineage but this impulse to drown myself? The sound of the water that runs through my sinus cavity when I turn myself upside down, maybe. My whole life I have been good, followed the rules, spoken kindly to strangers who stared at me. These days I want to run as far in the opposite direction of polite, calm, contained as I can muster.

PAPER LOONS

7 DEC.

I go mad because I cannot parse between here and not, beauty from violence, ice before it becomes water before it evaporates into the air. Chasing time, girl. I'm wrestling intangible wild things into a cage with the unwieldy, clumsy hands of physics. Nothing is solid for me, nothing constant. Rules and definitions, they dictate how we place ourselves apart from others, and I do not know how any longer. I look out at the world with a lens that never stops autofocusing between macrocosm and infinitesimal division. Boundaries are so easily violated. What is Above, what is Below? Before and After? They are invisible, social constructs we make with each other, no real power in them unless we believe. How do we keep things in, or out, if we are not strong enough to hold the line? My skin feels like that. My body.

Bailey and minor child report subject has not been seen since estimated 21:30 seventy-two hours prior.

OFF. FRANCES DELACROIX II: So you haven't seen her.

PATRICK BAILEY: No sir.

DELACROIX: Lena?

EMALENE ABERNATHY BAILEY: No sir.

DELACROIX: No sign? Sometimes when people go missing, and I know this isn't the first time Marietta's gone missing ...

BAILEY: No sir.

ABERNATHY BAILEY: Have you seen her? Have you looked?

DELACROIX: Well we've been busy, what with the blizzard.

· · · · · · · · · · · · · · · · · ·

80. A later report would list Ruin Lake as the *official recovery point* for the canoe. One of ten-thousand-some lakes plundered for ore and then abandoned in the development that swept the North Woods before the Collapse, Ruin was off-limits to me, to public trespass in general, but just west of its shores on a small Boundary Island made mostly of taconite, there was a transient community of radical limnologists, houseless folx, drunken, laid-off miners known as the Sons of Our Winter of the Great Divide. Though they did not wish to comment on this investigation, collectively they wished my mother well.

ABERNATHY BAILEY: You mean you don't want to look.

DELACROIX: No, Lena. But we've got to prioritize emergencies.

ABERNATHY BAILEY: You mean that man you found? Y'all think she can just magic herself out of a cell. She disappeared in the middle of that blizzard with no boots. Who went looking for her?

DELACROIX: We had a team.

ABERNATHY BAILEY: Who went looking for her?

DELACROIX: Ah, well. Ingrid—Ranger Solberg-Black. I was out around Ruin for a bit.

ABERNATHY BAILEY: For a bit?

BAILEY: Lena—

ABERNATHY BAILEY: No, Dad. I wanna know why they don't give a shit.

YOUR MOTHER HAD BEEN HAVING THESE DREAMS.

FLOODS
A FACE FULL OF WAVES
BEING STUCK UNDER THE ICE AT NIGHT.

PTSD

                              THE DROWNING,
                    I'D GUESS.

TRIGGERED BY WHO KNOWS WHAT—
ME,
MAYBE.

          THE WEATHER.

                    THE TIME OF YEAR.

IT WAS GETTING CLOSE TO THE SOLSTICE.

          Dad

IN SOME IMAGINARY, BETTER FUTURE, SOMEWHERE FAR AWAY

<hr>

HOME | 48° 12′ 57″ NORTH & 90° 55′ 23″ WEST

10 December 2016

Though she told me in her loon letters that I was not allowed to follow her, my mother began to instruct me more explicitly in the art of bringing Above Below, of preserving Before in a disappearing world of After.

`The doorway is easier to find,` she wrote,

`when the moon is at its brightest, or utterly, brilliantly absent.`[81]

`I cut a passage into the Inland Sea ice on a new-moon night, when the Ursids`[82] `were just beginning to blitz through the atmosphere above us. If you leave Collected things on the ice, I will come for them as soon as I'm able.`

`If you plan to search underwater, I always found it warmer to wear the black dry suit than the blue one. To strap the loon fins and headlamp on just before I`

. . . .

81. Hecate, goddess of borders, the One Who Hovered in the World Below the Living. It was in this Other World where she was known to be a liminal guardian, and why witches who worshipped her gave her names meaning the One Who Turns Away/Protects, the One Who Is on the Way, the One Who Is Before the Gate, and the One Who Holds the Keys.

82. Meteor shower between Dec. 16 and 26, visible strictly in Northern Hemisphere, as radiant (Ursa Minor) fails to clear the horizon or does so simultaneously with the start of morning twilight as seen from the Southern Tropics. Average of 5 to 10 per hour, usually at highest rate in late morning hours after moonset. Peak often on/around the winter Solstice.

sank myself in. Build a bonfire on the shore before you dive in, and you'll have hot rocks and embers for the bath when you surface again.

I've a stash of jars in the root cellar, and the instructions for capturing sound are taped to the inside of the record player. It takes a bit of getting used to, but you have gentle hands.

Take only as much as you can carry easily, and be careful you don't weigh yourself down too much without realizing—I don't know if I can come get you where you'll end up if you drown.

And so I threw myself into the task. From before sunrise to after sunset that night, I dove again and again into the ice, though I struggled to breathe. I filled the kitchen sink and the bathtub in our cabin with aquatic flora and fauna: deformed insects, diatoms like crystals in the water column, mussels buried in mud. I spent hours combing the wasteland of the Boundary Forests for anything salvageable, dragging the half-burned bodies of trees and ungulates and lichen across the isthmus, homeward. I draped mist-nets across the rafters, and our attic grew raucous with injured birds, chittering white-nosed bats that had fallen from their roost onto the snow, a slumbering hive of sickly bees from a rotten cedar stump. Scattered all across the tiny granite yard, I tended an ever-shifting assortment of shriveling herbs, saplings, drying mosses and fungi and weeds. To be kept and cultivated when, or where? In some imaginary, better future, somewhere far away, I supposed. I imagined her somewhere Below, wrapped in ephemera, trailing pieces of the world Above behind her.

Everything I left for her disappeared. I wanted so much to follow her, and wrote notes that said as much, but she warned me away.

Dad would be upset. Besides, he and Bea need you. I need you to keep looking for things for me to hide Below. Leave them where I can see them, and I will find a way.

She insisted the built microcosm should reflect beauty and ugliness alike, so I brought her orbs of rose quartz and cracked indigo bunting eggs, chunks of withering fungus, rotten garlic bulbs, roadkill.

Yes, she wrote on a blank white card, a plain three-by-five-inch piece of cardstock she left in place of half a bloody antler rack beside the shoreline. This. Bring me things that are broken.

But the work took its toll. I spent so much time in the cold, the slight jangle of water in my chest turned to a cough, and from a cough into a constant, singing hiss. From there pneumonia crept in, until it hurt to breathe too deeply and the entirety of my torso went cloudy, mauve and yellow.[83]

Still, it was Dad I really worried after. He had grown depressed, had long since stopped bathing, stopped shaving, and that night I found him fast asleep on the dock, covered in snow. When I put my hand to his shoulder to wake him, he was stiff to the touch.

"Mmm, yeah hon," he murmured, cold-drunk.

He could barely open his eyes, and when he tried to stand he nearly fell into the lake. I pulled him up and led him back inside to his bed. He curled under the quilts and I lit a fire, tried to heat the cabin so hot he couldn't drift into a Hibernation No One Would Be Able to Shake.

He groaned and rolled and tossed. I checked on him between dives; brought him broth made of winter leeks and grease, fermenting apple. His skin turned the color of summer cherries. He woke delirious and threw his blankets off. He stripped and bellowed, fighting some unknown dream. When I tried to help him back into bed he pushed me, knocked the Spotted

. . . .

83. I spat a hock of phlegm the size and color of a *cecropia* caterpillar into one of her jars, and left it on the ice for her. She never retrieved it.

One out of the way as he stumbled down the star-loft stairs and grabbed at the shortwave, yelling into the receiver

The breach is near to failing, watch the door, watch the goddamn door.

The Dogs started to howl at the static and he started to howl at their howling, and then I started to howl, too, because what the fuck else could I do, *I'm sixteen years old and I am alone* and none of that howling stopped until I snapped the antennae in half like a cricket's leg and the box went quiet and the Dogs went quiet and so did Dad except for the heaving.

"Nothing's falling, Dad," I said as I put him back to bed.
"The sluice isn't secured," he slurred.
"I'll take care of it," I told him.
"No," he said, bolt upright. "I won't have you going near the Mine."
                                        Then he vomited into his hands.
"I won't, Dad," I told him. "I'm not going anywhere."
"Good girl," he said, lying down again.   *My good girl.*

A fever spiked and he pissed himself that night. I was so afraid he was going to die I dragged him outside to cool him down, had to bathe him in the yard. The bathtub was full of Things I'd Found for my mother.

(cont.)

Um, I remember he was really aggressive sometimes, but in a weird, kind of charming way. After that first day, once he realized I wasn't going to tell him to back the fuck off, he pushed further. He'd play grab ass any chance he got, although I didn't take that real seriously because he did that with lots of folks, women included. But sometimes his jokes got pretty graphic, pretty specific. Made me think he was always about half a second from coming up to me and tearing off.

Tearing off. Like tearing off his clothes and fucking me.

What does that matter?

I'm not being contemptuous, I just don't understand why it fucking matters if I—

Yeah, I wanted him to. I wanted him to.

Uh, yeah I remember. Um, one day at work I went to piss in the woods, and he followed me. Came up behind me and slid his hand inside my shirt, across my stomach. Leaned in and let it linger there just below my—

Did I—yes. Okay, yes. Almost came in my shorts. Is that what you wanted to hear?

. . . .

84. See also: pp. TK.

Not in the beginning, no. We started hanging out a lot – ate lunch together, closed down the bar three or four nights a week that winter.

The first time—yes. I remember—why—Ms. Orleans, do I have to talk
about this?

—silence—

Fine. Spring thaw came, and he asked if I wanted to go fishing after shift.
Bring a couple beers, catch some trout, hang out on the boat or whatever. I met
him at the docks with a six-pack and he motored us away and we sat in the
middle of Ruin with our poles out and made small talk until sundown. We
were alone on the lake the whole night. Nothing happened at first.

He did. I thought maybe I'd been imagining everything. It was getting
dark, so I finished my last beer and I said, *Well I guess we better get,* and
I hauled the anchor up, but when I reached for the Evinrude he took my
hand and said, *Don't tell me you're gonna pussy out on me now, Olsen.* He
tugged his shirt over his head, climbed across the boat.

He did. He did.

No. I'd never even been kissed before. I didn't know. I couldn't hold my
hand steady to touch him, but he—

I don't want to talk about this. Do we have to keep talking about this? Ms.
Orleans?

EVIDENCE

Paper birch are easy, eager colonizers. Love to come in after a fire. All that sun, the fertile soil. A symbol of renewal. Their eponymous bark has been used for centuries to record history, to remember stories, but just as often, night after night, people destroy bits of these trees for immediate warmth. Paper birch is the best source you'll find up here, in this soggy land of lichen, sphagnum, snow. For this reason, they are also often associated with the underworld, the afterlife, the World Below.

—*Snow Birch Bird: A Natural History of the North Country*

Show me a small town that happily claims itself haven, its smiling brethren, its Godliness, its intimate anecdotes and communal memory gleaming, and then bend down with me and look closely. We will stare in upon its most terrible secret. Out in the open, there for everyone to see.

—John James Proulx, naturalist, minister of the
North Country Lutheran Apostles

He was too scared to speak up during the investigation, but he admitted it straightaway after the Fire. Once the skin grafts along his mouth healed up, anyway. His daddy asked if he knew her and the boy just started jabbering. Nonsense, but only somebody being willfully stupid wouldn't understand what he was saying. It's a funny man who stands and watches what he saw and then speaks honest about it, but I suppose we all assumed he had a kind heart at the center a' him. And I don't think we were wrong, not really. That's what makes him so confusing. Evil's easy to spot in a worm like Mitchum, but what does it mean for the rest of us if it can sit latent, quiet and unexpected, held to cruelty when the pressure's just right? Who are we if we make a man like Ellis Olsen?

—Jaybird Ironsen, cousin of Ellis

We are not all-knowing gods. Our ability to perceive outside of paltry sensory experience is minimal, even with a knowledge of maths. A parallel universe might exist, maybe many, even if only in our minds. And how magnificent is that? What rule says we cannot manifest them, as we have done with everything else in the human imagination? We are not all-knowing, but we are powerful. What might we need to build such magic? What desire? What destruction or violence?

—Dr. Jamuna Shrestha, *Awake in the World: Physics and Neuro-Philosophy for the Post-Electronic Age*

I wasn't part of it, I swear it. But Mine leadership did a good job of convincing folks they should bring her intentionally broken things, just to see if she could fix them. Just to be cruel. For some reason, most of these also turned out to be birds: a chick someone's fourteen-year-old son had plucked from its nest and thrown against the dirt; a pair of crows, their beaks tied shut by miner's metal. Old grocery sacks full of stolen eggs. A blue witch's warbler came to her tied to a length of fishing line. A man from the Mesabi mucking crew brought her a whole slab of cliff strapped on its side to the bed of a truck. *Three nests,* he said, and pointed at the painted rock swallows stitched to the rocks. And then there was that loon Mitchum brought her. Clearly just come off his shift—red earth all over him—but in his hands, he had the female trapped in a blue glass globe. He set the ball down at Mar's feet and laughed. *Sealed shut,* he said. *Good luck setting that one loose.*

—Frank Delacroix, Caelais Co. Aquatic Patrol, retired site chief, Mesabi Mine Co., Ruin Lake Branch

A MINOR ECHO OF MY WILD MAKER

November | Just a Few Weeks Before She Is Gone

She'd kept me home from school because she had decided the best way to teach me about the disappearing taiga was to put on a play.

"You don't learn the truth there anyway," she said. "Your science teacher thinks the earth is six thousand years old. You're a moose, and I am wolf. No, Lena—you're the North Country embodied. You're a vast field of snow, so cold, so solemn. You're everything to all of us, and if you go, we go, too. Lead the way!"

I didn't know where to start, new authority paralyzing. I had always seen myself in her, a minor echo of my wild maker.[85]

"Well?" my mother said, one hand on her hip, waiting on me to begin. Hair in a beautiful mess on top of her head.

But I had always just moved as she moved, and now she was asking me to go before her. And begin what? A revolution? A dance party? An expedition to the Arctic Circle? Any of these things could be possible. I felt so much expectation to play, to create, to break the rules she was always breaking, that I froze. I looked around the room. There was a can of paint under the sink, whitewash Dad had used for the outer walls of the cabin the previous summer. I opened the lid, slipped my hand inside, and held it up, dripping.

"If I'm snow," I said.

"My good girl," she crowed, and dipped her hands in the can, too.

We smeared it in circles, in great wide arcs, splattered it with flicks of

. . . .

85. Even that day, we were both wearing plaid pajamas. My hair is often tangled, too, and my heart easily bruised, mended, set alight again, sometimes so quickly that I am overwhelmed and have to squeeze every muscle tight to keep my body from exploding. I am beginning to understand, now, why she shouted and cried so often, the heavy weight of paradox that wore down her ration and reason.

our fingers. She disappeared into the star-loft and returned with a box of artifacts: birchbark, eggshells, speckled feathers, dried lichen, husks of pine cone. She took a handful and let it fly.

"We are creatures of the North!" she shouted. "We are moon junkies!"

I howled, put my hands on either side of my head like antler racks. I spun in circles with the paint can, a blizzard. Soon, she insisted we needed a larger stage, and dragged me out onto the lake, which was only just frozen over, which ached and groaned under our weight. The Dogs came along; the Wolf-Sister who ran along the ice as if she was trying to race the splits, the Shepherd Who Watches the shore for birds and lights and motion, the Spotted One who curled up at my feet whenever we were still.

Dad came home as the aurora borealis leaked blue-green light along the horizon. He warmed up cans of watery soup for dinner, lit a fire, ushered us toward the shore.

"Y'all have fun today?" he asked, side-eyeing my mother, the white paint smeared all over our walls. We shook the melt from our coats, our eyebrows. She grinned at him, kissed both his hands and his forehead. Her cheeks were like rose hips, and he bit her lip as she pulled away. Her eyes flashed a warm red, and I sipped the thin tomato broth and thought about how the North Country was melting farther and farther away, about the extinctions she was always so upset about. How many other worlds had disappeared that I would not ever learn about in school? How many other places would I never see? Together and cozy in our cabin, alone on our island way out on the Inland Sea, we fell asleep in a pile.

AN INCOMPLETE LIST OF THINGS MY MOTHER
BROUGHT TO THE WORLD BELOW[86]

[excerpt, specimen log from the Paper Moon Menagerie]

· 16 oz. North Country ice, latitude/longitude origins unknown

· 3 specimens of whistling black birch
(104 in. each, with root ball); 1 specimen each of spring, summer, and autumnal foliage

· 378 species of bird, including
> curling tail plume of magnificent spectacled pine bird (70 in.)
> 1 half the wingspan of colossal albatross (96 in.)
> 2 complete specimens of a nesting pair of fairy moon tern
>   (4 in. each)

. . . .

86. Though many of the records she kept have gone missing with her, she included several examples in the trunk I found on the shore. For other records, there are only descriptions: **Ex. (1)***Someone left me a box of glass spice canisters on the doorstep, each containing a different species of vegetable seed ready for planting, should the earth ever be amenable.* **Ex. (2)** *Beside the root cellar doors this morning, a hive of sleepy fire ants in a milk jug; a pair of tree swallows still in their nest and swaddled in a linen sheet; a baker's dozen jelly jars filled with lichen, moss, and algae. Folks are getting a hang of this collection thing!* **Ex. (3)** *Today I found the skull and spinal column of some small mammal. Left in the reeds near the dock, with apologetic chocolate cookies and a childhood fairy tale the leaver had created for the rodents who lived in their attic floorboards.* In another she describes a trumpet and its case having appeared in the yard, inside the bell of which was a living salamander and its brood. She says, *The note included was very brief, on a scrap of recycled textbook paper. "The drought has killed her siblings and all other ancestors. I couldn't think where else to keep her."* I don't know what metaphor the instrument was meant to imply to my mother—amplification, maybe, of the warning, the beginning she had been demanding folks pay mind. I noticed a change in her entries after that day, as if in some small way, the trumpet was bleating *You were right, you were right, you were right.* See also, *I am Dreaming of the Women Beneath: The Collected Journals of Marietta Abernathy.*

and the iridescent head comb of a flightless moor fowl (12 in.)
· 6 whole specimens of fish, including
    a pair of still-functional purple walleye lenses
    the tactile organs of a mature moss agate catfish (26 in.),
    and the speckled skin, pulmonary organs, and 1 preserved eyeball,
        freshwater eagle ray (30 in.)

· 2 pint jars containing diverse bivalve species' sperm and egg, separate and unfertilized

· 1 piece weathered cedar driftwood (85 in.), currently supporting
    a colony of commensal music-box eerie lichen,
    stink moss,
    and glitter-bomb algae, all unperturbed

· complete specimens, *singing blueberry bat* (2¼ in.); faint heartbeats found in 3 females, 1 male

· 1 box Marocaine mint ginger & lemon tea, actually containing ~ 235 sedated taiga honeybees, 1 queen, and the remnants of their former comb, including 32 oz. of honey

· complete specimen, little ghost loon, dark morph (22 in.); including a second set of pin, flight, and down feathers, and 1 hollow, empty egg

I KNEW WHEN I WOKE UP

HOME | 48° 12′ 57″ NORTH & 90° 55′ 23″ WEST

[excerpt, interview, Patrick Bailey]

You look just like her. Same eerie eyes, same hair. There's a glimmer on both of you nobody in this town can ignore.

Emalene Abernathy Bailey: What'sat mean, glimmer?

PB: Like a fish in the shallows—neither of you ever quite still enough to see clearly.

EAB: When was the first time you saw her? Do you remember?

PB: I came to Beau Caelais as a contractor on the North Country water line project, that first summer after you were born. I think I caught a glance of her a few times around town—at the QuikMart, down by the beachhead at a town picnic after the water had started to retreat.[87] First time I actually

. . . .

87. Known colloquially as *the Dryness*, a catastrophic drought that occurred spring 2000 to late winter 2001, immediately preceded by the Insomnia of Ashes. Freshwater limnologists and taiga ecologists refer to this as the first of the Anthropocene Collapses in the North Country. A hot, dry front blew in after the Fire, and the soil in the North Country baked and cracked beneath a haze of old ash, whipped up on a restless wind. The spring lakes of the Boundary Islands began to disappear, and even the water of the Inland Sea dried up. No rain fell, and what was left of the waves turned the color of bile. The shoreline crawled toward its low center as the lake evaporated, and the basin showed its face for the first time in a generation. The Water Shuttle shut down, and Dad joined a crew of laborers who funneled potable drinking water in cans from the clean wells north of the shore to Beau Caelais on foot. He says he was gone for days at a time. Bea has pictures of him: when he returns he is covered in foul mud, stiff in his joints and slurring, and when he rests, it is only for a few moments, slumped in a chair on the front porch with his eyes half open. They say he never complained, never once raised his voice to infant me or my mother, but in some ways I wish he would have. *Be angry,* I think. *Get frustrated.*

saw her though? She came to see me play at the Bear & Bird[88] one night and we walked out to Little Ghost on the dry flats afterward —hard to imagine when the basin is full, but in some ways I'll always think of the lake empty. Outta nostalgia, maybe. Bea had offered to babysit, I guess, so we stayed the night in a sleeping bag. I knew when I woke up the next morning.

EAB: Knew—

PB: —that she was the one.

EAB: Awww. Such a romantic, Dad.

PB: Cheesy, but it's true.

EAB: You are a bluesman.

PB: Given to great, consuming emotion.

· · · · · · · · · · · · · · · · · ·

88. In another life, Patrick Bailey might have been a touring musician. Though he only plays for me and Aunt Bea now, he used to sell out small venues, including the historic Caelais Crow Theatre. I am more surprised to learn that Hugo Mitchum once opened for him at the Windigo. "Played lazy pedal slide blues," Dad says. "Called himself Paul Bunyan's Boxers."

The Beau Caelais Daily

Premier Edition
The Island Sea: Today, sunny, a few afternoon clouds. High 87. Tonight, slightly more humid. Low 55. Tomorrow, sun then clouds. High

VOL. 1, NO. 1   Caelais County News for the North Country   YESTERDAY'S NEWS TODAY   www.beaucaelaistoday.com   *NIGHT EDITION*

FIRE AT MESABI MINE

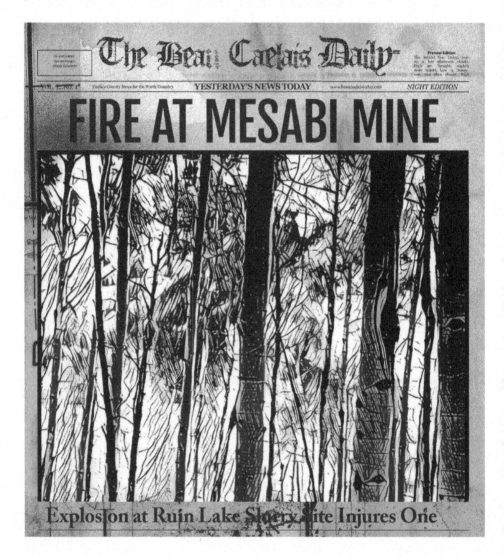

Explosion at Ruin Lake Slurry Site Injures One

THE WORLD BELOW, pt. II

HOME │ 48° 12' 57" NORTH & 90° 55' 23" WEST

20 June 2016—Six Months Until She Would Slip from the Jail Cell Window

My mother wanted to have a picnic.

"We never eat together," she said to Dad. "We never spend any time."

The next night, he came home early from the Water Shuttle with a string of sweet trout hanging in one hand, a basket of blueberries in the other.

"Where did you find those?" she crooned, a handful of the small, tart fruit already half in her mouth.

"Let's have a bonfire on the shore," he said.

My memory continues like this:

. . . she shoves a rose hip in her mouth and returns to the lake, dives again with a jar of blinking fireflies missing their antennae, a wing, a few limbs. She is gone ten seconds, then twenty, a minute, then two. My heart begins to pound in my chest—and then she surfaces again. The jar of fireflies is gone. She hauls herself ashore, loon-feather fins making her steps clumsy and loud. She leans over Dad, dripping lake into his hair while she kisses him. He looks up at her, at the moon.

I want to know why she left the jar at the bottom of the lake, imagine a collection of trinkets and secret artifacts like the cave of the mermaid in my favorite childhood cartoon. I know she wouldn't like it if I took something, but she is always bringing so much, I think *What's the harm? She'll never notice it's missing.* I take a deep breath and will myself to put my head under the water. I am not a strong swimmer; still instinctively afraid of what will happen if I can no longer breathe. I spend so much of my time Above being unable to breathe. Half-blind, submerged in a green-gray cloud of cold and wet, I kick my feet until my limbs burn and speed downward into the black of the lake. I ignore the buzzing colors sparking at the sides of my vision, kick down, down, until my chest begins to ache.

I won't make it   failure
what if I am too weak
failure   what if I don't make it back
failure   no air no air turn around
and then just before I flee toward the surface—

I find myself hovering above a place that is not a place; a bottom that is both solid and not.

There is no jar, but there is a hole: a shimmering tunnel that goes somewhere I will not understand until my mother is long Missing; where I will be afraid to venture because of what I might or might not ever find at its end. I lose the last of my oxygen in a cloud of bubbles, and before I am aware, I am Above again. The stars blink at me as I blink lake from my eyes. I gasp, cough, paddle weakly until my feet find muck to stand in. The fire cracks at the shore. I shiver, my blood all drained toward my heart in survival. I crawl onto the picnic blanket, wet, heaving. Dad wraps me in a towel and she asks if I am having fun.

"Where does it go?" I ask.

"Where does what go?" she asks, daring me to say more.

"There's a hole only I can find," she says to me later, after Dad has gone inside to bed. "Do you want to see the World Below? Do you want to meet the Women   Beneath?"

She gives me a pair of loon-feather fins and a headlamp just like hers.

"Swim down *hard*," she says. "As hard as you can, for as long as you can."

Then she dives, and I am alone in the dark Above. I try and I try to will myself to follow her, but when I try to take a deep breath in, I panic. Nearly vomit in my mouth at the thought of swallowing so much water, being so far Below I wouldn't be able to make my way back up. *What if I get lost on my way down? What if I run out of air?* I start to wheeze, and every accordion whine that sings of my lungs gets shorter and shorter and shorter.

I
DREAM
IN
BLACK
BIRDS
DARK
UPON
THE
SNOW

A
MILLION
FALLING

I
WAKE
&
STILL
THEY
COME

A
MILLION
CALLING
NOW

Hymn #13
Traditional Beau Caelais Spiritual

LIGHT RUNS IN THE NORTH COUNTRY

11 December 2016

I didn't sleep the night after Dad turned into the One Who Could Not Hold His Liquor, the One Who Almost Drowned Himself in Whiskey and Blues.

I lit all the candles we owned and watched him breathe, even though I was having a hard enough time doing that on my own. The Wolf-Sister paced and the Shepherd Who Watches sat sentinel at the foot of the star-loft stairwell, while the Spotted One slept with her nose buried at the base of my hip bone, clawing and whining in dream. To keep myself awake I hummed his songs; counted the time between his ribs rising and falling; counted the pine boards that lined the A-frame ceiling; cried.

He woke up around four thirty just like always.

"Hey darlin'," he said, yawning, when he saw me owl-eyed across from him. "Can't sleep?"

He was still driving double shifts for the Water Shuttle to and from the North Country and the Boundary Islands, so he had to be up before dawn just to make the beginning of his shift. For years I'd been waking up with him to share breakfast—oatmeal and dried blueberries, watery coffee—and that morning we ate in silence in the dark until it was time for him to leave. I followed him outside where the sky was low, humid and heavy.

"Off to school?" he said as he sat down and tied his boots.

"Soon." I still hadn't told him about what had happened with Rita Mae Mitchum.

"All right then," he said. "Well. Be safe."

"You too," I said.

"I'll be home before dark tonight," he said as he walked down the dock toward his Water Shuttle. "Maybe I'll bring us some good whitefish for supper."

"Yep," I said, though neither of us thought it was true.

He started the engine and let the boat circle slow past the shore. Chunks of ice rolled in against my toes, and I bent to hold it in my palms. Just as he caught the clutch and the quiet between gears hovered, he called out.

"Hey kiddo."

"Yeah, Dad," I said, looked up.

"Nothing," he said. "Love you."

When I went back inside, there was a paper diving bird resting on the windowsill of the star-loft with *LITTLE GIRL* written in black ink along one wing. I took the loon into the claw-foot tub and sank myself in with the fishes and snails I had rescued. The paper was thin and cold to the touch, as if it had been kept in an icebox, and inked with her favorite black-and-white feather pattern, its tiny, folded face staring with sharp red eyes. I unfolded one wing and watched the ink on its feathers turn into her words. Crease by crease, I unfolded the other wing, the tail, the spine, and watched the bird disappear into a letter. I read it once, and then I read it again. I read it a third time out loud, my voice bouncing against the roof of our cabin in my best imitation of her.

Dear girl: This time of year, there is so much light in the North Country, I could drown in it. I want to open my mouth and swallow all the sparkling mad world whole. I could just gulp and gulp until my stomach shone like a shadow box, but it wouldn't change a thing, there is just so much of it. I'm glad I won't be around to witness the winter; I feel as if my heart would break to watch the sun drain down the continent like that. Oh my darling, I wish you could see the lake from upside down. Next time, we'll go together, okay? Tell Dad not to be afraid. I'll be home soon.

I had no idea what *the North Country* meant if it was not here, what *upside down* meant. I folded the bird back up, slid it between the books on my bedside table, and wrestled myself into layers of flannel and wool, stuffed my feet into my warmest and driest and best ice-wandering boots.

In the dead of winter, the walk from Little Ghost over the land bridge is as exposed and cold as the surface of the moon, or so the weather reports in books of Before had told me.[89] The Storm into Which My Mother Had Vanished still had not ceased, though it was inconsistent and moody. Snow floated in a cloud doldrum; then wind would pick up and suddenly drive sideways into my eyes and nostrils and between layers of clothing. As I walked toward the mainland, I moved slowly, head down out of necessity, with a very small, inexplicable hope that I might stumble upon her. As I reached the mainland I looked back toward home and saw a wall of gray, lightning and snow building. My nose started to run, snot freezing onto my mitten, my hair.

At the library, I pored over old magazines from the World As It Was in an attempt to decipher where my mother might be. There were only certain places on Earth where it was cold enough to have snow cover and endless light, where the sun didn't always set. But it was the wrong time of year, almost exactly. Still, I made a list of places where these things were possible, and photocopied the corresponding maps from atlases. When I got home, I took the bird-letter out of the book, taped the maps to the wall of the star-loft, and marked my favorites with little yellow pins. I imagined my mother building houses of ice in the Arctic Circle. Racing sled dogs across the tundra. Dancing around the North Pole with her arms spread wide, smiling up to an everlasting sun. I read the letter again, and wondered where she would take me the next time she ran away, and what Dad and Aunt Bea would do while we were gone. I wondered

. . . .

89. In reality, the coldest temperature ever recorded on the moon is much lower than anything possible here, though perhaps the Anthropocene will see this come to pass. The lowest natural temperature ever directly recorded at ground level on Earth as of the time of the texts to which I am referring was -89.2°C (-128.6°F) at the Soviet Vostok Station on 21 July 1983; on the moon, the Lunar Diviner recorded a temperature of -247°C (-413°F) in a crater near the Mare Frigoris, or "Sea of Cold."

if I should tell Dad about the Hole in the Inland Sea. How long I would have to wait until *soon* came to pass, and she actually came home.

That night the sky was clearer than it had been for a week, and the moon turned the Inland Sea into a mess of loose ice that glittered and breached on the surface, undulating. After Dad had fallen asleep in his chair, I snuck back down the star-loft ladder, pulled on my mother's dry suit, shoved my feet into her loon fins, and went out to the ice again. I stood on the edge of the solid shelf trying to will myself in. *Breathe,* I heard her say in my head, *and just jump. Trust me, the chill will fade.* One huge whale-breath, and I kicked hard toward the bottom. The shock of cold was a vise around my ribs. Murk and silence, except for what spines of light the moon Above sent through the ice. Refractions rippled off lily-weeds and trout, the glass of my goggles. I thought I saw a form twist and beckon, and I kicked down harder. I thought I heard voices, singing. A flash of black-speckled white—the loon who escaped through the star-loft? I circled and spun where I thought the Hole should have been, but it was not there. She was not there, either. I kicked up and dragged myself onto land, let the air sting my cheeks red as I lay back and closed my eyes. Heaved air in. I gasped, swallowed, spit the Inland Sea out onto the ice.[90] When I opened my eyes again, the moon seemed suddenly low on the tree line.

Light runs in the North Country.

. . . .

90. Breathe, cough. Breathe deeper, cough and cough and cough. Wheeze, whine, whis- tle. Cough, cough, fight for breath, blue, breathe, wheeze, whistle, cough. Cough. Spit and bend, heave. Heave. Wheeze and heave. Cough and gasp and swallow. Bear breathe, wheeze. Chuff, cough. Chuff. Chuff. Chuff. Bend and heave. Blue. Breathe. Blue. Breathe. Heave, heave. Gasp and gasp for breath. Fight blue, burst, swallow air, and cough again. Hitch swallow halt and falter. Cough. Cough. Whistle. Fill and thistle, hitch, catch, hack cough panic breath gasp and cough and bend and heave. Reeve. Shallow, swallow, shallow, swallow. Wheeze wheeze wheeze. Breathe breathe breathe. Hitch and catch. Falter, wheeze. The water ebbs and rises. The water flows and falters. Cough, hitch, bubble, blue. Wheeze, whine. Whine, whistle. Breathe in and in and in—

I DREAM OF SWALLOWING ALL THAT WATER, GULPING

[excerpt, *The Collected Journals of Marietta Abernathy*]

21 October 1999

but Little Girl startles me awake and says

not yet not yet not yet

in my belly like a heart drum.

This world Above is weird and heavy, a wetness pressing down. That beat is awful, beautiful; the delayed snap of time sounding in my ribs; Mitchum's wrinkled pink balls on my thigh. *Slap slap slap.* Every day since. I wake with her, wake with his weight on me.

Everywhere I go, I'm
a storm
oppressive, a swath of hot,   red
blotches on the weather map.
Hail in the city big as peaches.
Tornadoes in three counties between here and the North Country
   land bridge, and
the constant spark of lightning flickering   on the horizon line.

Maybe it's Hell licking at my heels.
I don't believe in the Devil,
         but I'm nearly certain He believes in me.
I keep hoping for a tunnel back in time
            & I can't fucking find it.

The Inland Sea is drying up. Lowest water level since the Ice Age,
   or so they say. I am all mildew and   dust.

I think,   *Okay.*
I think,   *That's it,*
           I'm on my way out of this world.

So I'm ready to find that Hole and wallow, swallow, when Little Girl
kicks at my rib cage again and I realize I'm thirsty. What's a few more minutes topside? If I'm goin', might as well head for the Windigo.

But I glance in the abandoned sell-all store on the harbor on my way
into town and there she is—the One Whose Head Had Been Cracked
Open Like a Melon. Since I drowned I see the Women   Beneath
everywhere, and I've found her now, frozen in time at fifty-five, one side of
her head wet with blood.

She looks up at me when the door jingles, and I recognize the smile
from the photo they ran in the back of the papers ten years ago.[91]

It's good to see her back behind the counter, smoking cloves and

- - - - - - - - - - - - - - - - - - -

91. It went like this: Mariposa Walking Bear was a widow, proprietor, activist, and healer
who pissed off the State Housing Authority when she refused to sell her beachfront.
She didn't budge when the State tried to buy her off; the State Housing Authority
sued; the SHA suit got thrown out on precedent, some near-unknown treaty none
of them had ever intended to honor because, fuck it, *If nobody makes us, why bother?*
This might have worked for five hundred years before or ten months after, but unfortunately for them this was the Time of the Hon. Alice McKeig, a newly appointed
judge first of her name and her nation, first of the Women   Beneath to
sit on the North Country Supreme Court. The judgment against the State Housing Authority was entered and printed and mailed to all parties; Mariposa Walking
Bear won. Still, SHA didn't like that. Not more than ten days went by before Caelais
Co. sheriff deputies found the One Whose Head Had Been Cracked Open Like a
Melon in her own walk-in cooler. The County condemned the property; because
of the judgment, no one owns that strip of land or her general store but the Inland
Sea. See also: *Beau Caelais Daily* articles "Lakefront Condo Complex Controversy
Brewing," "Native Woman Wins Land Rights Appeal, County Housing Commis-
sion Development Plans On Hold," and "Walking Bear Found Dead."

finishing a crossword. The glass-front counter is clouded, empty except for a bottle of turned milk, her cigarette butts, and a pile of used-up scratch-offs. I wind my way between her looted shelves, grab a moldy map of the Boundary Islands from the floor, and ask the old ghost where I should go.

"Depends on where you want to be," she says.

"What are you doing up here?" I ask. "I thought y'all were stuck down—"

"Why you on the move?" she asks.

I pause. Not sure how to answer.

"I need to be not—not here," I tell her.

"Figurative or literal?" she asks. "Permanent transfer, or a temporary stay?"

A straight-faced question. Either way, would she have been surprised? I'm probably not the first to have asked her for advice of this kind.

"Both," I say. "Just a breath. Or a thousand. Something not this."

"New paradigm," she says, and I scowl, unsure of her meaning.

She points at one of two little ones running around in her shop, the Six-Year-Old Twins Who Were Stolen. Their energy is opposing: one smashes glass cases, spilling old bottles of birch cream soda all over the floor; the other sits quietly behind the counter on a barstool, red plastic toy binoculars pressed to her eyeballs.

"Stolen, sold, used up, and dumped," she says. "They're still new to this side.[92] Still get sad about the dividing line, so I brought them here to keep them occupied."

The quiet twin seems to ignore her, clicks and oohs, clicks and aahs, clicks:

"There's mountains in the middle of the ocean?"

"Sure is," the One Whose Head Had Been Cracked Open Like a Melon says.

Click.

. . . .

92. Raina and Ariette Valois, 1993–1999.

"So pretty!"

Click.

"Oh wow."

Click. Click. Click. As if impatient to see the pictures herself, Little Girl starts tapping her foot in rhythm against my rib. I wince, put a hand to my belly.

"Quit it," I murmur to her. "You're not missing much."

"Missing what?" the One Whose Head Had Been Cracked Open Like a Melon asks.

"Sorry," I say. "Just talking to myself."

"They're headstrong even when they're tiny," she says, and winks. "These two, they just love to travel. Car rides down 61. Canoe trips from their house to mine, asked for a sailboat for their birthday. Got dead instead. The toy binocs are nothing but thin paper wheels with pictures, but it's magic yet. Amplifies faraway things into view. You push that lever in and *click*, you're somewhere else again. Whatsat one called?"

Suddenly, the loud twin comes running over to their sister and snatches the toy away. They pull the picture wheel out and put it on the counter near enough for me to reach. "You can sorta see if you hold it up to the light," they say to me.

"Hey," their sister shrieks. "That was mine!"

"Hey," says the One Whose Head Had Been Cracked Open Like a Melon. "You'll each get a turn."

I hold the disc up to the ceiling light, peer through with one eye open, one eye shut to the halogen pulse of the store. I see:

> a blur of miniature sunset,
> a white triangle of sail,
> a rainbow of fish and fruit,

all surrounded by an unending sea the color of the walls in Sunday House.

I put the disc down on the counter. There is a stack of paper wheels and I pop another in.

Click.

"There's a whale in this one."

Click.

"And a shark."

Click.

"There's even an octopus!" the Six-Year-Old Twins Who Were Stolen yell in unison at me from a perch they've found in the rafters of the store. They throw plaster ceiling tiles down and laugh as they shatter, clouds of musty, black dust rising.

"If I were you," the One Whose Head Had Been Cracked Open Like a Melon says, "I don't know what I'd be lookin' for."

She turns to face me and I see the inside of her ruined eye, the teeth missing, the split in her pretty head where skull met asphalt and bounced. She holds my stare for a moment.

"How's the weather?" she asks.

She's put the clove between her teeth, pulls a drag, and blows out slowly through her nose. Already working at the crossword again. Keeping her good eye busy not looking at mine.

"Hot," I say. "Okay when the wind comes off the lake."

"Huh," she says. "Can't feel the breeze these days."

I leave the store, a blast of autumn heat on my face, and look out over the dry, dead lake bed. Stare and stare until I see it, that Hole Ursa showed me Below. I swear Little Girl knows as soon as I spot it, because she starts beating my bladder like a bell:

not yet, not yet, not yet.

I'm stuck on this path, this road, a boundary between Here and Thelre, Before and After. Below, I can rebuild all these dying islands. Bring back the pines and birches, the sphagnum and lichen on stone.

Next year I'd be seventeen, if I were still the one Ursa birthed in the snowbank, if I were not carrying this tiny heart inside. I'm not though. I'm caught between layers.

> Not quite one
> not quite the other,
> not both, nor either.

I'll wait until Little Girl gets here. I'll wait. But then I aim to stay put on the Other Side, if I have to fill my pockets with stones and sink.

THE ONE WHEREIN URSA ABERNATHY
CLIMBED UP ON THE MOON

THE BEAR & BIRD | 48° 3' 6" NORTH & 90° 30' 18" WEST

[excerpts, interview with Beatrice Orleans]

I haven't met any of the other Women   Beneath, at least not once
they've been—you know—beneath. The ghost of your grandma did come
to me once. Four nights and four days, December 1990.

She'd been gone for a while, so when she showed up in the flesh I was a little
freaked out. I went to the bathroom in the middle of the night, turned on
the vanity light, and she was there in the bathtub, soaping herself up with
my good bergamot oil. *Jesus, Mary, and Joseph,* I said. *Ursa, what the hell are
you doing here?* She smiled, got out of the tub, and hugged me. Easy, quick,
habitual. The way you greet a lover just coming home at the end of the day.

She didn't say a word that whole first night and the whole first day afterward. Thought I was hallucinating her, that maybe I was having a stroke.
Maybe I'd eaten some of my good mushrooms by mistake. But I could
touch her, feel her touching me. The air around her smelled like soft leather,
woodsmoke, butter and honey. She left wet footprints behind on the floor.
One of my Sunday House kids asked her if she wanted tea with her dinner
and she nodded, so I thought, *Well if other folx can see her.* In retrospect,
that girl had come to me from terrible violence; I don't know where she is
now, but I imagine she knows the Women   Beneath, too.

By day two, I thought, *Maybe this is my love-story-halloween-dream.* Call me
a cliché, that gay Gothic trope. Despite the doors creaking open at night,
or the cracked mirror, the too-fast rotting fruit, the drafty, settling sense of

unease. I don't believe in binaries anywhere else—we're far too beautifully messy—so I suppose I just didn't want to believe in a stark divide between alive and dead.

For three days and three nights, it seemed I'd got your grandma back. But out she came with it on the fourth: *The Ursids are coming. It's time to take my girl home.* The scar across her lower belly started to leak into the flannel she'd borrowed from me, blood all over her legs, all over the floor.

Shoot, she said. *Thought we'd have a little more time.*

She said we had one shot to sail straight off the edge of the Inland Sea.

You go get what we need, she told me. *I'll meet you both on the beach.*

So I gathered up what I thought would keep us safe us wherever she meant us to go: a Zodiac, life jackets, dried fish, a thermos of hot cider, all the blankets I could find. Your mother was last, most important.

Marietta was seven, still living with her father the Hunter in Ursa's old cabin on the banks of Ruin just shy of the Mesabi company line. I snow-shoed out there in the middle of the night and took her. It was easy: he was a dead drunk, didn't stir. I breathed her name into her hair and she wrapped herself around me like a toddler, like I'd been carrying her around like that her whole life. I wished I had. I brought her to the water and laid her down in blankets on the rubber heart of that blue boat. Head soft on her yellow PFD, as was required by North Country law.

The Ursids are coming, Ursa said, sitting beside me.

I was a wonky navigator, but your grandma was a ghost, so what other choice did we have? I revved the engine, drove until the gas ran out. After that I paddled and paddled us out into the middle of the Inland Sea. Have you ever been to the middle of the Inland Sea? Dark dark dark. There is no darkness so black, entire. When we were lost from every direction, I stopped. Ursa at the prow, Marietta asleep at the center. The whole of the Milky Way above us. Shooting star after shooting star. It was so cold. My breath made clouds. Your mother breathed and her water heart turned it to snow.

You ever been to the moon, my dear? Ursa asked. It was near new, a halo of cobalt barely visible.

Not in this life, I said to her, and she winked. Started huffing hard into the sky—air into ice. She breathed and breathed until she had built herself a ladder, and then she started climbing into the sky.

The Ursids fell. One, two, three at a time. Streaks of light—tails like strings of electric rope—and your grandma reached for them with her hands. She grabbed and caught and leapt, clambering her way from one brilliance to another until she was miles above us. The ice and the stars and their tails melted behind her. She got smaller and smaller until all I could see was a slight twinkling against the night.

What a view, she called, her voice tinny and faint like we were using an old metal cup and a wire. *You're so beautiful.*

Marietta was still asleep in the belly of the boat.

How are we supposed to follow you? I hollered.

Can't hear you, Bea, she said. *A little louder.*

How am I supposed to bring your girl up there? I yelled.

Still can't hear you, my dear, she called. *Keep her safe for me awhile longer.* [93]

I still look for her shadow every new twenty-eight days. Maybe this is what I mean, to be a moon junkie.

. . . .

93. Every year on the winter Solstice, the Ursids smatter and fizz across the sky. They are the only bright things in December, some of few interstellar beings still visible to us below the perpetual haze that is the sky in After, and the meteors paint us and the world for three nights in mystery, dreaming. Every year when they began, my mother used to tell me their stories as we watched them from the great, round window in the star-loft. She said they were our grandmothers returned as birds; told me how far they had traveled, unimaginable distances like *light-years* and *thousands of millions of miles*. I asked questions: *How long would that take me?* and *Who else have they have met on their way?* In the morning, I'd wake to a breakfast of tiny soft-boiled eggs; Aroniapancakes; fragrant wintergreen tea; a jam of juniper and honey. It is still my favorite holiday.

SUSPECT INTERVIEW: MARIETTA ABERNATHY
OFFICER FRANCES DELACROIX II, BADGE #1875902
LOCATION: CAELAIS COUNTY JAIL
DATE: 1 DECEMBER 2016
TIME STAMP: 20:56–21:07

OFFICER FRANCES DELACROIX II: We found him on Ursa's land.

MARIETTA ABERNATHY: Oh, so it's hers now? I thought it belonged to Mesabi.

DELACROIX: You know what I mean, Mar. Where were you last night, this morning?

ABERNATHY: Out.

DELACROIX: Out?

ABERNATHY: On the Inland Sea, yeah.

DELACROIX: Anybody with you? See you?

ABERNATHY: The Women   Beneath.

DELACROIX: Who?

ABERNATHY: You know some of 'em. Donna[94]—she's your niece, right? She was there.

----

94. Donna Gunnarsson, daughter of Linda Delacroix, 1981–presumed dead 1996. Last seen hitchhiking near Beau Caelais South down Highway 61, likely headed toward the Little Iron Mesabi Site where both of her parents worked.

DELACROIX: My sister's kid? She's dead, disappeared, what, like fifteen, twenty years ago?

ABERNATHY: Women don't just evaporate, Frank. We don't just *dissolve*.

DELACROIX: We looked. I looked. I was on the search party. She was nowhere.

ABERNATHY: I think you know, Frank, there's folks don't want her to be anywhere.

DELACROIX: Mar, you gotta tell me what happened to Hugo.

ABERNATHY: What happened to Hugo?

ALL THE LIGHTS ON

[excerpts, interview with Beatrice Orleans]

Ellis comes in sometimes when it's storming. I gather the wind and thunder scare him. Here's as safe as he's likely to find in Beau Caelais. Never does drink. Never asks for any food, but if I've got the ingredients I bring him a grilled cheese and a chocolate milk. Think he likes that. Eats the sandwich like a little boy— everything except the crusts. He sits in the corner booth by himself, watches folx love on each other. Mostly they ignore him. Better than what happens when he's in town, I guess, but still I feel for him. I don't know if he's ever been loved on before.

I think it's easy for this town to forget he used to be something else. Even as a child, he was the size of a man. Now all anybody sees is that eye, the shining scar across his jaw. The jibberish. *Moon bones* and whatnot. Did you know he stayed at Sunday House with me? For about a month, late in the spring of 1999.

I remember him like I remember all my kids—frozen at whatever age they were when they came to stay with me. So to me, Ellis is just turned seventeen; clumsy as fuck and constantly hitting his head on the underside of the doorframes, having gained fifty pounds of muscle and grown eight inches in about a week. Hair the color of raw pine. Sweeter than a maple tap. Cliché as it is to say, he always did remind me of a puppy.

He showed up at Sunday House at about two in the morning, soaking wet in a pair of boxers and his work boots. Shaking, visibly injured—bruises just starting to rose across his ribs, abrasions on his palms, his chin. I'll never forget the way his face twisted when he tried to sit, because that's when I noticed the blood running down the backs of his legs. Wouldn't go to the doctor. Wouldn't let me touch him, but I got him to lie down in a medicine bath before he curled up on the floor of my bathroom.

He slept on that floor for another six days. All the lights on. I wrapped him up in one of my granddad's old army blankets, and he pressed his back to the wall farthest from the door. Day seven he moved, but he didn't speak for another week.

Then finally one morning he came downstairs while I was making breakfast. Asked if he could have scrambled eggs. Ate almost a dozen before he cleared his throat and asked if I could keep a secret.

"Sure can," I told him.

"Okay," he said, and swallowed hard. Looked up at me and then back down at his hands.

"Hey kiddo," I said.

"Yeah," he said.

"You can tell me," I said.

"Uh-huh," he said. "I know."

"Hey kiddo—"

"Yeah, Ms. Orleans?"

"You're safe," I told him.

"Yeah," he said. "I—uh, I know. I guess—I guess I'll just say. Uh, my dad, he found me—caught me and Hugo Mitchum, um. In one of the Mesabi boats out on the lake. We were—we weren't wearing—he threw me out of the boat, took me home, and told ... he told my brothers to beat the faggot outta me in the yard. So, um. Yeah. Please don't tell anybody I told you. Hugo doesn't want anybody to know."

I kept his confidence, and I stand by that. Forcing folx to report doesn't reckon healing. But I never will forgive myself for not trying harder to help him believe it wasn't his shame to keep.

THE ANTHROPOCENE

the most violent

the Anthropocene

the Anthropocene   story

a people with

awareness of

an empire   their greatest might

their doom

A people   at

the center of   precarious universe   cos-

mic

black out

blossoms,
blasts of sound,

bloom cluster

The humble

bound.

aries between

the emergence

or the disappearance of another,

harnessed here

to uproot

the hearts and minds

in wonderment

Technicolor

We   starve.
the birds and the bees   the bats
the butterflies   we eat
we   give

our lives   dictated

by the wind," []

YOU'RE JUST LIKE YOUR MOTHER. SUCH A FUCKING
TEASE, TITS ALL PERKY.

Rita Mae Mitchum

WE ARE A MORBID BUNCH, THESE DAYS

HOME | 48° 12' 57" NORTH & 90° 55' 23" WEST

14 December 2016

Without explanation or notice, a series of new letters appeared in the middle of the night—in the star-loft, in the icebox, on the shore. It was as if she'd reached through some hole she'd made in time or space to place them just where I might find them.

One floated up behind our house in a bottle, the glass clouded in algae and lotus roots.

```
The Women        Beneath want to meet you. I tell them
how curious you are, your eye for detail and light;
they think you would be good for our dusty bones. We
are a morbid bunch, these days.
```

Another fell from the roof in a nest of straw and hair, the paper was crusted in guano.

```
Do you remember when I used to show you where the
Ursids would crash into the lake if you wished for
it hard enough? The stars on this side seem closer,
somehow, like they're just about to plunk themselves
down into the ocean. I'll bring you a little cosmic
fireball to keep by your bed in a jar.
```

I found tiny feathers and a small white card curled in the egg carton;
a long-winded tale about lunar bodies taped to the back of the
mirror;
botanical drawings with annotations slipped into the books on our

shelves.

In all of them she claimed to be building something in the World
Below.

Soon everything Above will be gone, dear girl. But
don't worry, we'll be safe down here. When it's time to
go under, you'll have everything you could ever need.

I wanted to tell her that she was what I needed; that Dad and the Dogs
and Aunt Bea needed her, too. She didn't hint at why she had disappeared,
or why this time it seemed unending. I set all of her letters in the steamer
trunk, beside the loon still trapped in her blue glass globe. The bird had
stopped calling, sprawled limp and dull-eyed; the only sign she was still
alive was a faint cloud that fogged the glass when she breathed.

The Hole in the Inland Sea flickers in and out, she'd say
as an apology, or, It's hard to predict when I can come back
across.

As if that made up for all that Lost, all that Missing.

I AM DREAMING OF THE ONE WHO SLEPT & SLEPT BENEATH THE ICE

[excerpt, *The Collected Journals of Marietta Abernathy*]

3 October 2016

and it's becoming too much. TOO MUCH

when I'm awake, the pull of the water is faint, but I   shut my eyes and
  I can't keep him

                                        breaking
                                        in.

This morning, he is   a great white cur   all fur,
skin creased in a range of ice, mountains that I climb and
climb   without end. When he roars, the sound fills the space
between my bones, it   rattles me open. The smell of   h i m
folds around me like a quieting avalanche,   like dead lungs.
He laughs; the bedrock, the core of the earth   r i p p l e s, the snow on
my shoulders and my con ti nen ta l   thighs begin to melt away,
my   human face a mask, I croon   at the melt,
                                    I can't stop
                                    singing

a song I don't   really k no   w.
A cloud, dark   birds arrange themselves in my hair. I try
  to keep myself   together
the melt splits me   open,   loses all that w e i g h t ‖ w a t e r ‖
  w e a r y ‖
I have been carrying   . I spill and spill   and spill, until?
                                    what is left:
                                    the glaciers are g o n e.

we have   lost

every
calved   berg,
moulin river,
every. blue. inch.   of floating
land over horizon
named

Arctic

the North

Country, the space we revere

we are our own undoing

the Inland Sea lost   when we say
thank you
and
I'm sorry
and
we mourn how
the Anthropocene brings us here, we mourn
you and your dying

ice.

In this dream: I come   to a house   my home   but   he
follows me through every door, a growl rolling from his throat like an
Evinrude. I shut myself in b l u e

a room filled with snow to hide

but he burrows through tiny grains of   shell and   glass and
stone glinting.

I crawl
through
a window

and find myself outside
Sunday House, knocking at
its demolished door. I keep
trying and trying to put
something between us but
there is nothing solid to keep
him from coming. I run

into a grove of   dead birch leaning hard against a   heavy wind
      run run run down the road toward Ruin and   see

the One Who Was Left Sprawled in the Ditch Down Highway 61.
      They float under the icy surface of that ditchwater   with their
      eyes tilted up .

A silent yell   pools at the back of my throat
                              when they turn their face toward me,
                              when they   open their mouth.

I wake up. A pane in the star-loft window has cracked, and the wallpaper
      beside my head has curled and warped at the seams. Everything is cold,
      except for Patrick—I put my hands to his face and he is warm in a way
      that is no longer familiar. The radiator is still on, still tink-tonking with
      hot pressure from the inside, but it is useless against the cold I've made
      around us. His breath hovers over his lips, a sweet cloud. He snores, rolls
      into me. Sometimes I think he can tell.
The floor is wet. It gives and moves beneath my weight, like the Inland Sea
      itself is under us.
These white lines I've left behind, they're telling. Witness to where my
      brain has been wandering.

The Beau Caelais Daily

HEADLINES
Not any longer
- Frank Delacroix

Premier Edition
The Inland Sea: Today, sunny, a few afternoon clouds. High 40. Tonight, slightly more humid. Low 5. Tomorrow, sun then clouds. High

VOL. L. No. 1   Caelais County News for the North Country   **YESTERDAY'S NEWS TODAY**   www.beaucaelaistoday.com   *NIGHT EDITION*

LOCAL TEEN DROWNS

ABERNATHY GIRL COMES BACK TO LIFE

Mesabi Mine Co. Reports Indicate Foul Play

THE ONE WHOSE WILD & QUIET FOLLOWED
THE WATER

THE BEAR & BIRD | 48° 3' 6" NORTH & 90° 30' 18" WEST

[excerpts, interview with Beatrice Orleans]

December 1999. Mar'd been staying with me at Sunday House, belly getting bigger and bigger with you. The night before the Fire, the collection vanished and her Paper Moon Menagerie flickered and stopped functioning.

There were so many people waiting with their specimens, winding in line for miles. They didn't know the Hole had closed, of course. Nobody had ever seen it but her. But it was gone, and there they waited, all along the edge of the Boundary Islands north of town, along the shrinking lake bed and into the center of Beau Caelais. Camped out, standing, in small groups or alone. All eyes turned toward her. They came forward and she took their bird bones and their shriveling pines and their rocks and their melting ice caps and their watercolors. They went home, wherever and however far away that might've been. They got to go home. But the next day, we woke to a shadow over Beau Caelais. Black flies falling en masse from the sky.

I remember her that morning: shining, dry, like a brittle bird bone left at the bottom of an oven too long. About to break. Those flies were small as salt grains, but there were millions. Death buzz hummed low, constant, while they spun and twisted like drunks, dropped and flipped on their backs and wheeled at the air until they slowed, twitching, finally still. Where one died, there were many.

We closed our windows to keep them out, but it didn't help. They fought through fine-wire window screens and crawled under doorframes to gather and die at light bulbs, faucets, the little fuckers. Air was dizzy. She kept telling me she'd heard reports that the Collapse had gone beyond the Boundary forests to the Yellow Sun grasses hundreds of miles south, across the Sky-Reaching cordillera to the Very Edge. Her collecting habits had been growing more and more obsessive in the months since the Solstice—she'd long since stopped doing anything else, even sleeping—and with all those new deposits she could not take Below, things were piled up on each other in the yard, on the beds, in the bathroom medicine cabinet and the kitchen pantry. That day, she was more frantic than I've seen her before or since, manic as she strung rope from anything tall and strong enough to hold the weight of containers, hung cages and nets that creaked and reeled with creatures folx had asked her to save. Sunday House still had a few other kids staying there, and I didn't really know what to tell her, tell them.

Mar, I said. *They need to sleep someplace, too.*

We can share, she said. *Everybody's used to it.*

But the flies piled up, too.

*Bea, would you, I need—can you—*she stammered at me, a rag in her hands, waving at all the jars and bulbs and buckets of broken life dusted in tiny corpses.

I need to clean this up. I can't—and I only have so much time. They're all gonna die, stuck—

Then she knocked over a glass terrarium filled with mosses and a clutch of baby snakes whose eggshells had been contaminated. She'd been so nervous they wouldn't survive, so happy when they'd finally started to emerge. *There you go, babies*, she'd said. *Safe now. Safe now.*

ut exposed to the cold winter air, the snakes writhed like worms on the hook.

Shit, she said, wild and quiet. *Shit.*

I saw the tizzy, tried to distract her before she spun out. *Hon, come eat something*, I told her, one hand on her back. I brought her inside to the breakfast table, a bowl of mushy oatmeal and thrice-used-teabag water. She sat at the edge of the chair, barely breathing.

Maybe you've done enough, Mar—I told her, and that was my mistake.

Sometimes, in a moment like that, there's not anything anybody could've said that *wouldn't* set them off. All that practice, years and years of talking to kids with trauma written all over 'em—but sometimes I misread, overstep, really put my foot in the shit. And they let me know when I do it.

Marietta dropped her bowl on the table, got up, and slammed the door so hard a piece cracked from the frame.

Maybe this doesn't concern you, Bea, she hissed at me through the crack. *Maybe you don't know what needs to be fucking done.*

Then she was gone, walking out onto the dying basin of the Inland Sea on her bare feet. Ice and black flies be damned. I remember her face in the glass so well. So well. She was practically feral by then. Like I'd hit her, or trapped her in a cage and she'd just accused me of being in charge of the keys.

Frank says he saw her later that day, walking toward Ruin with those loons on her head. Heavy bag hanging over her shoulder.[95]

. . . .

95. See also: pp. TK.

(cont.)

As many details as I can remember. Uh, his mouth. Everywhere. It was everywhere.

Where? Uh—My neck, the—the inside of my thigh.

Uh, yeah. Yes. Yes, he did.

Do *you* remember the last time somebody sucked *you* off?

I made a sound like a bird when he took my cock in his mouth. You want me to re-create it for you?

No. Before—he flipped me on my hands and knees. Pressed me into the bench, and shoved something hard so far inside it felt like he'd split me in two.

No, I didn't want that.

No, he didn't ask.

No, I—I don't know. I wasn't ready, if that's what you're asking. I told you. He didn't say *I'mma fuck you now, Ellis.* He just did it. It just started happening.

. . . .

96. See also: pp. TK.

He's about five nine, five ten.

I'm six four.

I don't know, maybe fifty, sixty pounds.

Yeah, I get that I'm bigger than he is. You don't believe—? You don't believe me. I didn't want—I didn't—he's a strong motherfucker. He's been work- ing for Mesabi since he was fourteen years old.

No, I didn't know he was gonna do something like that. I just told you I'd never even been kissed. No.

Doesn't it matter he's older than I am? Isn't that against some law?

Um, he bit the back of my shoulder. Left a red ring of teeth.

What?   I did. But I didn't want—

When he—when he put his hand on . . . yeah, I, uh. I came all over the bottom of the boat. I remember the smell—my cheek was pressed against the bottom. I saw myself. I remember the smell. Old aluminum, algae, rust. Fish belly.

I mean I didn't want to. Or maybe I did, but not like that. I mean, it felt—I don't know. I'm confused, it's confusing. I didn't—can I take a break? Can we take a break?

PAPER LOONS

15 December

Lena baby,

they will call you all kinds of dirty things
wield words and weapons against you
point, threaten, holler.

I hope they do nothing worse, but it has happened to
others and I think you are old enough now to know the
truth of it. They will do everything they can to stop
you, to make you small, to contain you.

We have been dragged from our beds in the nighttime,
by angry folks with torches waiting.

We have been thrown in holes,
tied with ropes,
locked in boxes and cells,

but you will learn their boundaries are not your own.

Find a way through when there is none.

                    Make windows of walls.

The Beau Caelais Daily

Premier Edition

VOL. 1...No. 1   Caelais County News for the North Country   **YESTERDAY'S NEWS TODAY**   www.beaucaelaistoday.com   *NIGHT EDITION*

LOON WOMAN

LOCAL EPHEMERA COLLECTION HOAX?

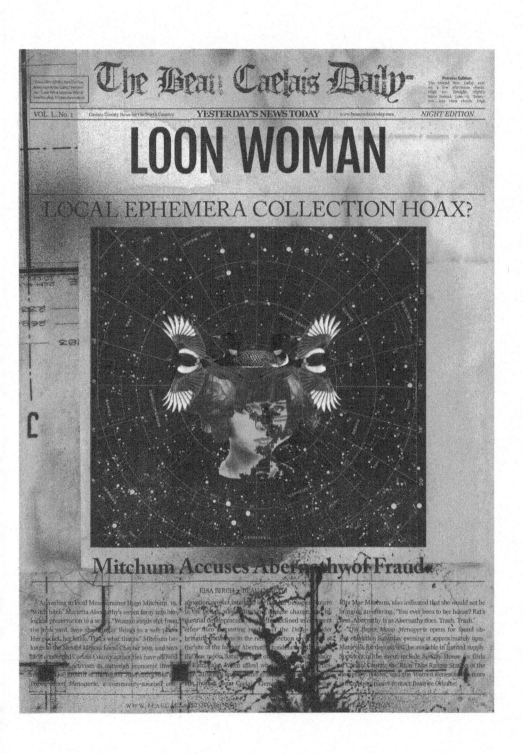

Mitchum Accuses Abernathy of Fraud

LISA BIRCH, DEALS DESK

According to local Mesabi miner Hugo Mitchum, 19, "witch bitch" Marietta Abernathy's recent foray into biological preservation is a scam. "Woman steals shit from the junk yard. Says she's takin' things to a safe place. Her pocket, her kettle. That's what that is." Mitchum belongs to the Mesabi Miners Local Chapter 209, and says he is concerned Caelais County authorities have allowed her activism to outweigh economic investment. Preservation Menagerie, a community-sourced con...

...struction project intended for future biological future in the face of plastic pollution, climate change and industrial development... declined to comment... other than contesting... of the *Daily*... bringing donations to the new collection... the site of the former Abernathy residence... this... the Loon moon. Saturday night... Rubin Lake, when asked wh... although located on... the... Beau Caelais Elem...

Rita Mae Mitchum, also indicated that she would not be bringing an offering. "You ever been to her house? Rat's nest. Abernathy is as Abernathy does. Trash. Trash."

"The *Paper Moon Menagerie* opens for found objects collection Saturday evening at approximately 9pm. Materials for deposit will be available in limited supply. Sponsors of the event include Sunday House for Girls, Caelais County, the Ruin Lake Ranger Station of the North... Walks, and the Women Beneath... more information, please contact Beatrice Orleans.

BOYS WILL BE BOYS, RIGHT?

Frank Delacroix

EVIDENCE

Everyone who stayed through the winter couldn't get a lick of sleep because of the sounds—the Insomnia of Ashes. Folks said they saw three mad dogs up and down the shoreline of the Inland Sea—the shepherd, the spotted mutt, and the wolfish silver bitch. They were seen playing with fish in the middle of a frozen lake; walking on their hind paws through stands of burnt cedar; running in front of traffic and then disappearing into thin air as soon as headlights were dimmed.

> —Frank Delacroix, Caelais Co. Aquatic Patrol, retired site chief, Mesabi Mine Co., Ruin Lake Branch

Ellis Olsen, 17, of Beau Caelais, was found by wildfire crews near the wreckage of the Mesabi Mine Co. Slough Office three days after the Ruin Lake fire ended. Though his injuries are rumored to be quite severe, anonymous sources in the Caelais County Burn Clinic report he is expected to survive.

> —"Ruin Lake Fire Leaves Devastation in Its Wake," *Beau Caelais Daily*

He ain't a man. Not any longer.

> — Walter Black, former bartender at the Windigo

Emotional repression is inherited up here. Ya grow up tight-knit and slightly incestuous, quick both to defend the town's honor and to spread toxic gossip, proud of your ability to thrive through frigid, half-year winters and industrial environmental blights. Avoidant, maybe. Small towns make themselves into a language, and there is no way to learn it other than to pass time inside the babel.

> —Lisle Bergstrom, Caelais Co. Executive, 1989–present

That rotten smell? Sharp, kinda sweet. Nauseating, like wet fat sat in a dish overnight. Smell of him sticks in the air. Sticks to me. I smell that on me every day. Do you know what it feels like to smell like that? But he's *good*.

Good. Good. Good-at-heart. Good. All anybody ever says is that word. What does that even mean? Doesn't even sound like a word anymore. After what Hugo Mitchum did, what he watched Mitchum do? No.

—Excerpt from official transcript, *Caelais Co. Case No. 1999CF0328: State v. Mitchum*

We are the shadow's ribs, thick silver poured in the division between air and time. We are the first ones to find the sun. Our bark blisters with memory, and when we shed our skins, history litters the loam. We feed the lace-winged and the horned foragers. We give our dead over to consumption, spores that wake hungry in wet summer. Our heads bend and shimmer, our golden seed falls and paints the webs of spider mothers. For millennia we have carried you through the waters in our bodies, your weight held by our hollowed spines. For millennia, we have been felled and burned and made into ash, and we have always returned again. We are that strong, and that precarious. But it was a Fire of fires that left us moaning. Our skins burned first, quick like nightfall, like frost.

—The Birches

Singing hey oh / Swimming hey oh / Sinking hey oh / Watch me sink deep / In the water.

—Hymn #13, Traditional Beau Caelais Spiritual

AN INCOMPLETE LIST OF THINGS MY MOTHER
REFUSED TO BRING BELOW

though some men tried to force her:[97]

fragile bulbs filled with light pollution,
sulfur smoke

a puddle of condoms,   sticky in cum

jars of copper slurry runoff
that rising stink of Mesabi's foray farther and farther into the North Country;

cups of undrinkable waste: rain left in the wake of excavator weight, frothy
   like pressed coffee; the murk of nitrogen
and fat lingering
on the surface of the CAFO pond down Highway 61,   sweet and terrible
grease.

earth from the wide, empty stretches of land remaindered
witness to murder, Boundary timber.

the bones of broken-down machinery
scavenged from Ironsen's dumping ground

neither
the rusted pins and gears of a 1987 state trooper cruiser,
nor
their rifle stocks, empty magazines, cracked sights, ball bearings, or pistols
   painted with art deco roses and the names of the officers' mothers.

. . . .

97. *you cunt, see what comes*—handwritten note affixed to a crate full of spent casings;
   found at the foot of the Paper Moon Menagerie, c. April 1999.

She took loose tobacco and juniper liquor but left
the packages of rolled cigarettes
and cans of Hamm's on the shore.

Someone gave her a pile of dog shit.

That,
she returned to sender
                              in a paper bag   on fire.

BEAU CAELAIS PUBLIC LIBRARY, MICROFILM
#0078336

[In Solidarity with Survivors]

Birth and death records my mother collected and stored in a coffee tin above the bathtub in the star-loft, all for people I would come to know as the Women Beneath. Most of the twenty-some pages were unreadable by the time I discovered them, words obscured by blotches of blooming green-gray mildew and fogging, milky plastic. Badly damaged, the images on the roll are blurred as if it had been submerged or left out in a rainstorm.

In Solidarity with Survivors of Sexual Assault

In ▮▮▮▮▮▮▮▮▮▮▮▮▮▮▮▮▮▮▮▮▮ solidarity with survivors ▮▮▮▮▮▮▮▮ many ▮▮▮ came forward ▮▮▮
their names ▮▮▮▮▮▮▮▮▮▮▮▮▮▮▮▮▮▮▮▮▮▮▮▮▮▮▮▮▮▮▮▮▮▮▮▮▮ and violence.

Nell ▮▮▮
▮▮▮ Sampson
Nettle ▮▮▮
Grace ▮▮▮

S. ▮▮▮

Anna ▮▮▮

▮▮▮ Bancroft
▮▮▮ Gillespie
▮▮▮ Waters

Bjork ▮▮▮

▮▮▮ LeFey
▮▮▮ Ewan
Frankie ▮▮▮
▮▮▮ Fernandez

Anderson

▮▮▮ Killjoy
▮▮▮ Barner
Emmalyn ▮▮▮

Skunk ▮▮▮

Leah ▮▮▮

▮▮▮ Valkyrie
D. ▮▮▮
▮▮▮ Alexandria

▮▮▮ Gaya
Snow ▮▮▮

▮▮▮ Tsolkas
▮▮▮ Renata
Sofia ▮▮▮
Gigi

Rose ▮▮▮
▮▮▮ Barbara

Rae ▮▮▮

For more information ▮▮
or if you are in need of support, please ▮▮▮▮▮▮▮▮▮▮▮▮▮▮▮▮▮▮

▮▮▮ 24-Hour
▮▮▮ Hotline: 1-800 ▮▮▮▮▮▮▮▮▮▮▮▮▮▮▮▮▮▮▮▮▮▮▮▮▮▮▮▮▮▮▮▮
▮▮▮ survivors. ▮▮▮▮▮▮▮▮▮▮▮▮▮▮▮▮▮▮▮▮▮▮▮▮▮▮▮

▮▮▮▮▮▮▮▮▮▮▮▮▮▮▮▮▮▮▮ hold accountable
those who have perpetuated harm, ▮▮▮▮▮▮▮ dialogue
about consent, ▮▮▮▮▮ transformative justice, ▮▮▮▮▮▮

▮▮▮▮▮ Collective ▮▮▮▮ survivors of sexual
assault ▮▮▮▮▮▮ their own healing ▮▮▮▮ alternatives
to the legal system ▮▮▮▮▮ seeking safety and justice.

▮▮▮ perpetuated sexual assault ▮▮▮▮▮▮▮▮▮ hold
them accountable ▮▮▮▮▮▮▮▮▮ meaningful change

support groups ▮▮▮▮▮▮▮▮▮▮▮▮ crisis intervention, shelter,
▮▮▮ advocacy ▮▮▮ survivors ▮▮▮▮▮

▮▮▮▮▮▮▮▮▮▮▮ experiencing civil or criminal charges
▮▮▮▮▮▮▮▮▮▮▮▮▮▮▮▮▮▮▮ community accountability

▮▮▮▮▮▮▮▮▮▮ Bi, Trans, Lesbian and Gay
▮▮▮▮▮ end violence ▮▮▮▮▮▮▮▮▮▮▮▮

▮▮▮▮▮▮▮▮▮▮▮▮▮▮ survivor leadership, community
organization and public action. ▮▮▮▮▮▮▮

▮▮▮ Sexual Violence ▮▮▮ Center. ▮▮▮

FUCKING FLIES UP HERE.

                BLACK, TINY, BITING.

                                  SCOURGE OF
THE NORTH WOODS.

ONLY GOT WORSE AFTER WHAT HAPPENED TO YOUR
MOTHER.

A
PLAGUE
ON
BOTH
YOUR
HOUSES.

Frank Delacroix

I AM DREAMING OF THE DARK, OF THE BLINDED WIFE WHO SHOWS ME THE WAY

[excerpt, *The Collected Journals of Marietta Abernathy*]

21 June 2000

It is hard for me to believe it has been a whole year.

I look at my hands, and I don't recognize them; they are not mine. To be truthful I look at the world Above and I don't recognize anything, anymore.

I drowned, and swallowed so much water I drank the Inland Sea entire.

This morning I give my little Emalene to Bea and leave; the Dogs follow close behind. I cross the isthmus to the lake floor. It's been six months since I let the Fire run, and now Beau Caelais and the Boundary Islands are white in ash, save the charred pine and new shoots of paper birch, a sea of hot pink fireweed. The flowers wave their heads in the wind and I smell nothing but singe, sugar.

When I reach Little Ghost and look out over the dry bed

its whiteness burns, a flashbulb

and in this moment i am empty   of memory and rage; blinded.[98]

Little Girl came to me on a cold morning, and then the Dryness came after her. I don't know what else to call it, because the water is gone, and the

. . . .

98. **blind** / blīnd / (adj.) used to describe one who cannot see; (v.) to deprive someone of sight. From the Old English *blind*, "destitute of sight," also "dark, enveloped in darkness, obscure." See also, the Old Norse *blindr* and Gothic *blinds*, perhaps, via notion of "to make cloudy, deceive," and from an extended Germanic form of the root *bhel,* meaning "to shine, flash, burn."

Hole at the bottom of the Inland Sea is gone with it. All that remains is a scar on the earth, a faint circle of black glass incongruous against the expanse of the lake bottom. I wonder if maybe I have imagined everything—the longer there is nothing, the more I think it might never have existed at all.

The only thing I can think is to dig my way back, so I take an old cast-iron shovel to the Hole and swing it high and hard above my head until I am drenched in sweat. Each strike rings

first: sharp hammer against iron tie

then: low vibration, harmonium

                                    hammer!   harmonium
                                    hammer!   har mo ni um
                                    hammer!   h a r m o n i u m

but no matter how many strikes I make, still the Hole stays closed.

Fuck, I shout. *Fuck fuck fuck.*

My voice rips, and what birds still live in the emptying biome burst into flight from their perches. I can't see them all but I know they are buzzing, screeching, smashing themselves into window and grid wires and asphalt to escape the sound.

Fuck, I shout again, and swing.

Sparks fly. The Wolf-Sister growls at the ground like it's done something to her grandmother. The Shepherd Who Watches paces and paces, and when the Spotted One whines, all three of them start to bark and snarl. But then a voice comes from behind me.

            Mar,   *let us have a try.*

I turn to see the Women   Beneath standing in a line, the sun running down the horizon behind them.

"Where did you come from?" I ask.

The One Whose Head Had Been Cracked Open Like a Melon takes the shovel and starts swinging. In unison with every strike she yells *ha* and then *ha* and then *ha* again, teeth bared like a bear's. Slowly, a crack grows across the Hole. *Ha!*

The Six-Year-Old Twins Who Were Stolen have birch sticks in their hands and coronets of fireweed in their hair, and while the Loud One runs off and disappears across the empty basin of the lake to play fetch with the Dogs, the Quiet One plucks the flowers off her head and makes me bend to take her crown.

"You do not have to be good," she says.[99]

I don't know what she means. She takes my palm in her tiny ones and she gives me a stone.

"This one is yours," she says. "Don't should on yourself."

Dusk falls around us, and the One Whose Head Had Been Cracked Open Like a Melon still swings and yells and swings and yells, the crack across the Hole now blinking at us all like the eye of a nebula. The One with a Necklace of Handprints puts a hand on my shoulder.

"Hungry?" she asks.

"Fuck yes," says the One Who Was Left Sprawled in the Ditch Down Highway 61.

"I didn't mean you," says the One with a Necklace of Handprints. "But I suppose I can make some for everyone."

Then she reaches into her mouth and pulls feather moss and kindling from the soft of her throat; reaches again and pulls a pack of matches, lights a fire; plucks rainbow trout from the air, still wet and squirming as if she's

. . . .

99. *You do not have to crawl on your knees / for a hundred miles through the desert, repent-ing.* M. Oliver, 1986.

found some seam in the Universe through which she can reach. They roast and crisp and we eat them when their scales start to shine.

"Where's Ursa?" I ask between bites.

"She's Below," says the Blinded Wife. "Keeping watch."

The sky is black and starless and the white of the lake bowl glows. The Loud One comes racing back with the Dogs close at their heels. The One Who Was Left Sprawled in the Ditch Down Highway 61 lies on the ground and makes angels in the calcium ash, and both the Six-Year-Old Twins Who Were Stolen lie down next to her to make angels of their own. They roll and giggle, sit up and face each other and paint their cheeks with white lines and dots. It is near midnight when the Blinded Wife stands up, hands out to steady herself, then opens her mouth wide, white-toothed, and wails like a loon:

ahww-ooo-oo oo-oo ooo oo-ooooo

ahwwww-ooo-oo ooo-oo ooo-ooo

"Figured I'd try echolocation," she says. "And it worked—I can see you all now."

She wails again and again and again, and one by one we join her

ahwwww-ooo-oo ooo-oo ooo-ooo   ahwwww-ooo-oo   ahwwww-oooooo-oo ooo-ooo   awwwhhooo

ahwwww ooo-ooo   ahw-ooo-oo, ahwwoo ahwwhooooo oo-ooo ahww-ooo-oo, ooo-oo, ooo-ooo

ahwwww-ooo-oo, ooo-oo, ooo-ooo   ahwwww-ooo-oo, ooo-oo, ooo-ooo

Back and forth and back and forth, until even my bones vibrate. The Blinded Wife finds her way to the shovel in the darkness, and she takes it by the hilt.

"Watch this," she says, and swings at something she cannot see. The eye of the nebula in the Hole of the Inland Sea splits wide

. The water trapped Below starts to rise.

SPIT IT OUT

[excerpts, interview with Patrick Bailey]

Emaline Alfred Bailey: When did you know about Hugo?

Patrick Bailey: What do you mean, when did I know—

Him and Ellis. You worked with them sometimes, right? In the North Country?

Everybody knows everybody on the Line.

So you knew—

I didn't know Ellis, not really. He was just a kid. Brand-new, never really got started. Never came back after the Fire. All I ever knew about Hugo is that he was an asshole.

That's not what I mean, Dad.

Well, then what do you mean? Spit it out, hon.

Him and Ellis Olsen. I didn't know they were together.

If you're talking about what I think you are—what Hugo did to Ellis—they were never together. Hugo may have *fucked with* Ellis, pardon my French.

How is that different—

Hugo was a predatory, homophobic prick. What Hugo did was never about affection, attraction.

BEFORE THE FIRE

CAELAIS CO. WILDERNESS SERVICE, RUIN LAKE
BRANCH | 48° 4' 15" NORTH & 90° 39' 19" WEST

[excerpts, interview with Deputy Ranger Ingrid Solberg-Black, Ruin Lake

Station]

We year-round residents in Beau Caelais were a bit like a dysfunctional family. Town had an October-through-June population, approximately four hundred. That number grew every summer with campers, hikers, lake-admirers come from South to visit while the weather was pleasant and we had daylight. In the dark winter months, we were joyful, stoic bastards, communal in suffering. We had conflicts, sure, and we started to see more and more with economic downturn in the timber, the fish, the mine. Money was tough. Fights broke out sometimes, but we kept to ours. Aside from those prone to slurring over whiskey at the Windigo.

HUGO WAS BUILT LIKE A GREYHOUND
INCLUDING, I HAVE BEEN TOLD,

                                            THE

                                            PINK

                                            PENCIL

                                            DICK

                                            THAT DID

NOT ALWAYS COOPERATE

      Aunt Bea

OFFICER RESPONSE REPORT
DATE: 18 JUNE 1999
LOCATION: WINDIGO BAR & TAVERN
OFFICERS SORENSEN, LIGHT HEART
TIME STAMP: 18:43–19:07
CHARGES FILED: DISORDERLY CONDUCT, DISTURBANCE
OF PEACE

OFFICER LIGHT HEART: Mr. Mitchum you need to calm down.

HUGO MITCHUM: Oh fuck off, Birchbark.

LIGHT HEART: Excuse me? Birchbark. Is that supposed to be offensive?

OFFICER SORENSEN: Hugo, knock it off or we'll have to take you in.

MITCHUM: It was all that tree-hugging cunt's fault. This fucking thing she's got going, it's fucking Devil shit. She's a goddamn witch and y'all don't do anything about it. It ain't right. Who gives a shit if the blueberry bees fucking die off? I gotta work, don't I? I gotta eat.

SORENSEN: That's true, Hugo, but—

MITCHUM: Why isn't she in handcuffs yet?

SORENSEN: We're gettin' there, Hugo. What happened? Tell us your side of the story.[100]

MITCHUM: She stands out here every damn day, yellin' and shoutin'.

. . . .

100. "The legal system is designed to protect men from the superior power of the state but not to protect women or children from the superior power of men." —Judith Herman, *Trauma and Recovery*.

LIGHT HEART: So you're saying you didn't do anything to instigate.

MITCHUM: What the fuck you mean, instigate

LIGHT HEART: You didn't say anything to anger Ms. Abernathy?

MITCHUM: I didn't say shit. Bitch is always pissed about something.

THE ONE WHO LOST CONTROL OF HER THROAT & HOWLED[101]

THE BEAR & BIRD | 48° 3' 6" NORTH & 90° 30' 18" WEST

That summer of 1999, seasonal tourism in Beau Caelais had begun to suffer after a group of children from a nearby camp disappeared in their canoes, reports of glowing eyes and high-pitched moans in the vicinity. The Collapse had taken its toll: the water in the Inland Sea was historically low.[102] Rain clouds hovered and then dissipated without relinquishing their stores; ice from the glacial steppes in the North Country receded, melting and evaporating under punishing heat. The Boundary Islands and their lakes dropped farther. Fishmongers ran out onto the dry beds to scoop dying fish into baskets. Birds and reptiles began to abandon their eggs, and mammals dropped their babies early or stillborn or both, more than a few local women included. The only industry left to exploit was the mineral deposit, and when the Mine was done, the North Country looked a flayed carcass. Bloodied and laid bare.

Walter Black, North Country old-timer, father of Ingrid, and former bartender at the Windigo, tells me the air-conditioning was out one

. . . .

101. In public no less, and *How dare she?*
102. From the same date in *I Am Dreaming of the Women   Beneath: The Collected Journals of Marietta Abernathy.* "A moonscape of lost objects has been revealing itself as the water goes down. Things I've found this morning alone: amethyst and abalone beads, calcium plates, bones (human and otherwise), two giant rusted anchors the size of tractor tires, shirt buttons, shell casings, twelve mismatched socks and at least as many soles, a mound of disintegrating diapers (used), fishing hooks, unidentifiable teeth, what surely must be miles of tangled net, three piano plates but only eighty-eight keys between them, a full bottle of McGoggins (twelve-year) miraculously undisturbed, and a turquoise 1979 Ford Pinto with a blind seven-foot-long catfish living in its engine block. Who knew the Inland Sea was also a beautiful dump? For fuck's sake."

unusually warm early summer evening, and the Mesabi crews were having their pre-shift Hamm's and hot dish.

"You could hear the sound of Marietta yelling through the open windows. *Copper miners are cowards. Iron miners are nothing but moose shit!* So Hugo knocks his barstool backward and asks me to pour him a double shot of whiskey."

"I says, 'I will not,'" Walter tells me, crossing his arms in staunch re-enactment. "So the Mitchum kid spits in my face. Runs down the rickety stairs to the parking lot before I could kick his ass out."

He says the whole bar heard Hugo snarl a string of obscene things to my mother.

"Then there's a thump and a bunch a' cursing, but by the time everyone emptied out into the parking lot, Marietta was already on top of Hugo, her hands at his throat. Snapping her teeth inches away from his nose."

Witnesses claim her arms and legs reeled at the air as Ellis lifted her up and away. They say the big Swede tried to reason with my mother, to apologize for Hugo's untoward behavior, but his hulking frame coming up from behind must have seemed like an attack.

"Marietta kicked Ellis hard in a location most vulnerable, nearest her eye level," Walter Black tells me, winces in remembered empathy. "Bellowed and buckled over, went down and stayed. Felled like a hundred-year-old pine."

TATTOO
MY
NAME
ON
THE
BACK
OF
YOUR
TONGUE

SPEAK
LOUD
MY
NAME
TILL
I
WAKE
FROM
THE
LAKE

Hymn #13, Traditional Beau Caelais Spiritual

SO MAYBE I KNEW THE DIRECTION I WAS LEANING

HOME | 48° 12′ 57″ NORTH & 90° 55′ 23″ WEST

[excerpts, interview with Patrick Bailey]

A few weeks ago, end of November. It was the middle of the day and you were outside on the lake, thank fuck, whatever small grace exists. The short-wave channel was open, buzzing but quiet. And then suddenly, a voice.

Full moon tonight, girl. Been swimming lately?

I recognized his voice but didn't know how to place it. Even thought I'd imagined it at first. But she went stiff. Bent over, got down on her hands and knees. Threw up a stomach full of something that looked like curdled milk.

I mean, I'd never say this to Frank—maybe I shouldn't even be saying this to you—but fuck Hugo Mitchum. I'm glad he's dead.[103]

She'd just sort of found good ground—no nightmares, no hallucinations. She'd been sober for years. I don't know how he found the channel. Only Bea knew we were using it.

Mar said he was just a prick who lived with his mother in the woods. Said

. . . .

103. Patrick Bailey rarely expresses anger, though when he does, it's usually when he sings. Hoarse from the work, the lack of water, his voice is gritty, more growl than mourning. These days, he refuses the lighthearted songs I still want to hear. Instead, he picks old-timey politicals, historical myths, and ballads, a few local spirituals that show their subtle, violent roots when he barks them out on his resonator all night long over the lake bed. "The Slow Ghost of Ogallala," "Dust Bone Blues," "Lord of an Empty Land," "A Hundred Years of Rain Couldn't Bring Me Home to You." Hymn #13.

she wanted to end things on her own terms. *In my own time.* He may have been a skinny, strung-out, unemployed idiot, and she certainly had reflex, brute rage, and strength on her side. I knew enough about what had happened between them to know better. To trust that he was capable of more than he seemed.

Or maybe I was afraid of what *she* was capable of doing. I mean, if she was aiming to bury a body somewhere out in the Boundary Islands—well, I'd made up my mind the moment I met her. I'd follow her anywhere.

To help her or stop her, I'm not sure which.

I guess I went and loaded the gun.

So maybe I knew the direction I was leaning.

SCAR TISSUE

[excerpts, interview with Beatrice Orleans]

After you were born, your mother got all kinds of weird shit for the Paper Moon Menagerie, even though she'd announced its end in newspapers, over the shortwave. It was the moon junkies who couldn't stop bringing her things. Once or twice a day, some of them hand-delivered by a *handsome* man from the Water Shuttle.[104]

A sweet old queer from the North Country sent her the bloodied wings of a mossy starling, feather by feather in individual envelopes. Absolutely no explanation but their name.

Another sent her the dust of Inland Sea agates that had been ground down on a diamond wheel. *Found these in Gran's well*, said a note on the recycled jelly jar. *Mesabi took control last week.*

Folx who held their hurt and folx who couldn't figure out how to keep it— they all started giving it to her. She got a box of desiccated butterfly scales from a water pilot whose plane was grounded by the fuel shortage; the otoliths of three ancient blue catfish, submerged in a jar of maple whiskey by a femme who had once spent her life traversing the Boundary Islands in her great-grandfather's handmade canoe, but who had been forced to anchor her boat when her route grew clogged in slurry; the skull of a juvenile black bear, gifted to her anonymously by someone who claimed to be related to your grandfather. But the deposit I remember most was Ellis Olsen's.

. . . .

104. Patrick Bailey, the One Who Carries Us to Shore Like a Wave.

Mar and I were eating dinner on Little Ghost. You were brand-new, about the size of a hot potato in the crook of my arm, and she was making Ursa's one-pot stew recipe by the fire when he came up the dock out of nowhere. I remember thinking: *He must have walked across the lake.*

It was still chilly, late April, but he wandered up the beach in nothing but an oversized flannel, a pair of giant snow boots, and his skivvies. All ribs, skin paper-thin like spring ice. In his one good hand, he had a single speck-led brown egg about the size of a chicken's.

Dark moon coming, he mumbled. Knelt, placed the egg on the ground by her feet. *Ruin loons gone upside down.*

It was hard to understand him, all that scar tissue marled across his mouth. The burns on his face had only really just started to heal and he was clearly ashamed of them, because he would not make eye contact with us. He stood up and turned to leave, but he lifted his eye just enough. Saw you, stared like he'd been lost in the dark and somebody'd turned on a floodlight. Took a step forward.

You need something, Ellis? your mother said. Hackles.

That egg sat in a butter dish for about a week before it started to smell. She said she couldn't bring herself to deposit it with the rest of the specimens. A few weeks later, I found it broken open on the beach. Dead twin chicks inside.

I AM DREAMING OF THE ONE WHO COULD NOT
CONTAIN HER TIDES

[excerpt, *The Collected Journals of Marietta Abernathy*]

22 June 2016

I woke up in the bathtub. Water pouring from the faucet, spilling over the sides of the basin and across the floor.[105]

Now I'm lying here on my back, staring through the star-loft, counting the constellations. Pleiades, Ursa Major, Corvus. All the windows are open and I can hear the lake.

I'm scared. Not because I don't know what I've done, but because I know it won't be the last time I won't know it. That I've done it before and forgotten. That I'll do it again. What if this is not the last time I open my eyes to realize I cannot explain why I feel like I've been submerged, like I'm still submerged somewhere far away?

After the Fire, I could still see where the trees had been. I mourned on them for weeks, even long after the embers were all that I'd left. Hadn't meant to let it go on like I did, but I found once I'd started it that a sour, twisted

. . . .

105. She writes here of how the water wouldn't cease its looming at the edges of her mind. In retrospect, I think it was on/after this date she started to build the cabin Below. She'd been bringing things to the Women ___ Beneath for almost sixteen years, but she had no place of her own. Pieces of our home Above went missing that summer. The huge plate-glass lake-view window that made up much of the southern face of the cabin disappeared, as if it had been ice melted by the sun. Our pantry shelves, once cluttered with ceramic dishes, old pots, drying herbs, and other garden ephemera, had been emptied. The kitchen table blinked out, and all four ladder-back chairs went afterward. In my memory, the bathtub in the star-loft had always been filled with pristine lake water she'd made safe from contamination, but slowly that drained away, too. Bit by bit, she was carrying the World Above, Below. See also: pp. TK.

part of me was happy to watch the world curl and burn like newsprint by a match.

My birch friends my pine souls my cedar people, they were not the objects of my disaffection, but I was not dexterous enough to guide my anger, just strong. Didn't realize how strong I was. Am. Still some days I feel it seeping out of my fingers, and I know what I am capable of when I take the ash in my hands. This is why I need to be with the Women   Beneath. The water would keep me cool and hazy, drown this spark of injury in me.

COME BACK

19 December 2016

Each night Dad returned long after sundown, soaked, hands red and stiff from the lake wind. We were both exhausted, unwilling to admit it. Bless Aunt Bea for offering to stay out on the island.

"Just a few nights a week," they said to Dad. "Figure it's better she have somebody around to check on her."

We all knew they were there for both of us.

We existed in orbit around each other. He seemed close to becoming untethered; if my mother was the Loon Woman, he was the One Who Loved Her, the One Who Swam Out After Her and Carried Her Back to Shore. Who was there to swim after him? The longer she was Missing, the more obvious her Missing became. Without her there to take the specimens to the World Below, our cabin reminded me more and more of a kind of morbid shrine, both to her and the things she had been trying to save before she disappeared. Four nights in a row, I dreamt a thunderstorm spit and cracked at the horizon, and a high wind shuddered the ribs of the cabin. I heard Dad's hushed voice, and saw him moving my mother slowly through the room as if she was sore, having trouble walking. His hands clutched at her shoulders, ushering her toward the bathtub. She was naked, shivering. Wet, from the storm outside? Her skin shone, speckled black and white. It must have been flashes of lightning, refracting through rain on the glass. Or was it? He helped her into the bath and she crooned, nonsensical. Then she would be there beside me in bed, ready to deliver the paper loons by hand. *Up, up, a little bit higher,* she'd sing into my hair, just on the edge of consciousness as I stirred, confused and bleary. *Oh, my, the moon is on fire. Come, Emalene, in my flying machine*—When I woke fully—wheezing in the dark—she was gone. On the fifth night, I tried not to sleep at all. Stayed awake hoping I would catch her creeping through the cabin, climbing in through the hole in the star-loft window we had yet to repair, despite the eerie whistling sound, the cold, bitter wind. I wanted to follow her, and I had whole conversations with her in my head where she'd tell me that she wanted me to come along, too. I left notes for her in place of those I had found, hoping they would reach her. I sent word out into the Inland Sea, and waited. *Come back.* But she did not retrieve my letters. The papers wore thin, the ink faded. The bottles settled and rode the tide, rocking and rocking against the shore *come back* until the glass cracked, and the letters fell out *come back* and turned to pulp, unread, *come back* unopened. *Come back.* I fell asleep, and when I woke up after dreaming again, hers were there waiting for me, and mine had been left behind.

I TURN MY BACK ON YOU AND THE INLAND SEA, MOTHER

HOME | 48° 12' 57" NORTH & 90° 55' 23" WEST

19 December 2016

(Yelled into a jar and thrown into the lake,
where it sank to the bottom and may/not have fallen into her World
Below)

The Inland Sea is   ice tonight,   a roof over that
    unfathomable hole, deep as a blink,
a millennia's worth of   d i s t a n c e   between
        here
and   the place you would not name,
    where you say
there   we Women   Beneath will go
    when you/I/we/us am/are done, but you are not done and you are there
and not here, though you said you would   make tracks
come back   leave a line
come back   draw a map
come back and   *even when I'm lost*
you claimed I could   walk through after you. Liar. I can   not
    because you
do not
exist, and I do not exist   without you. The hole you made, you filled
    it   in   when you decided
to leave me behind   tell me   you could not stay   any longer.
    How
do I follow you now? I can(not) walk
through water, through walls, through time and space
like you   said.   Liar. Liar. Liar. This is the beat of my
                                too-hard heart.

173

Do you hear it   pulse   on the Other Side
the same as I could hear yours   from within?

You/I/we/am/are ripping   at the joints,   You/I/we/am/are
   stiffening, my ribs turned to iced birch branches   after   a squall in
December.   We are   paused, not quite living, maybe not dead.

Your jars of diatoms, your
wall of water caught, contained, protected
from   marauders who would do
   you/me/we/us harm. Your
aviary of extinct   birds,
the tank of white   whales bears piano bones

the flock of fairy terns   you kept in your hair
                                 with the fruit bat and the river locusts
all those pearled mussel shells and curling
fiddle ferns,

                    the elkhorn coral you kept in the pepper
shaker,
                                              the underwater
lilies, bleached and pressed with your   rice and the   lavender and
   saffron
between the pages of the letters you sent   from
   wherever you went;

all of it, so precious, you said.   What is left of a world that no longer
   exists
so you went back in time
        through holes
        you made

to escape   to navigate   to remember   to covet
to keep   to save.
 Save what? All you did was promptly   forget
about me/you/I/us
so I did what you wanted
I   flew rebel   yell.   I listened only to myself.

 I will not look at the water.

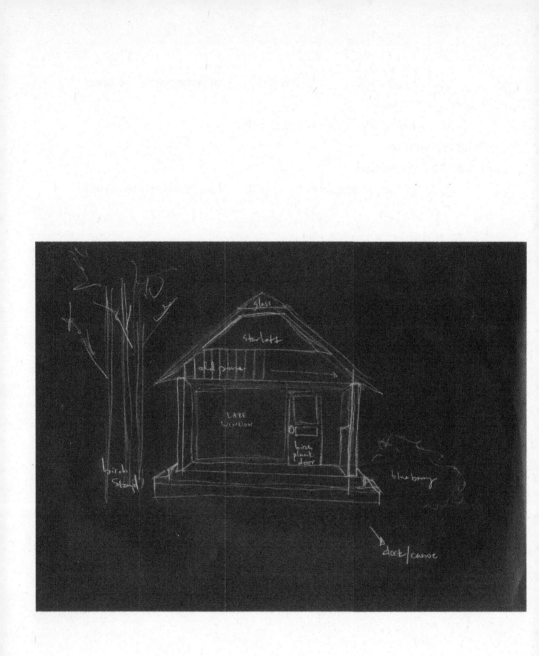

I STILL HEAR THAT SOUND SOMETIMES

CAELAIS CO. WILDERNESS SERVICE, RUIN LAKE
BRANCH | 48° 4' 15" NORTH & 90° 39' 19" WEST

[excerpts, interview with Deputy Ranger Ingrid Solberg-Black]

Nobody slept from December to June of the following year because the whole forest creaked at night. Well, the place where the forest used to be. I was in the Army before my post at the Wilderness Service, and some of my squad lost limbs. They talk about nerve damage, phantom pain—well I think these burnt-out stumps, the root left behind underground, they had this same kind of trouble. Their branches and their leaves and all the little flowered buds that come in springtime, they weren't really there any longer but they still *hurt*. I go out on duty now, walk the border of the lake and where the woods used to be. Still hear that sound sometimes.

After the Insomnia, we made a myth of her. Turned her into a creature, part ghost, part bird, a thing drowned and come back breathing. It wasn't her who brought a blackness down on us. We all stood by, we all watched. We knew the truth, and didn't do enough. She was a little girl. She was a little girl.

Now, nobody knows for sure but them, so I can only tell you what I've heard ... but I'll repeat that much at least, lest it be forgot and that boy truly gets away with things. I came to take her statement at the hospital. Part of the Ranger job. Held her hand while they stitched her up. A wretched mess, but she didn't flinch once. I'll tell you what I remember her mentioning, but it's been near seventeen years.

THE ONE WHEREIN URSA & AUNT BEA GOT MARRIED ON MAGNETIC ROCK

THE BEAR & BIRD | 48° 3' 6" NORTH & 90° 30' 18" WEST

[excerpts, interview with Beatrice Orleans]

It was a new moon at the stroke of midnight, Friday the thirteenth of December. Coldest day of 1985, maybe sixty below with the windchill. My happy tears turned to frost on my lashes; your grandma told me my eyes looked like they were rimmed with stars. People always say she was a battle-ax, but god, what a sap. My maple sap. We walked through the pines arm in arm, and before absolutely no witnesses, we swore to keep each other safe, warm. *Tonight, we dance in the snow,* she told me. *Tomorrow we march on the mine.* And dance we did—with sparklers, in snowshoes. A clumsy, hilarious waltz.

The Hunter was besotted with her, as were we all, but he understood she was mine. Or at least I thought he did. I understood theirs—it had been a one-night stand between them. She got pregnant and she thought about doing something else, but there weren't a whole lot of options in the North Country—then or now—and she decided she did want a baby, after all, accident or not. She didn't mean to stick with him, too, and I thought he knew. He'd have rights, but that didn't mean they were a couple. The Hunter had other ideas though, I suppose.

When she—when the rangers found her on Mesabi with her belly—he told everyone it was the Mine. He told everyone it was him who had found her. But he came stumbling out of the pines with blood all over his hands—I found her. I found her. I didn't have the nerve to speak against him. If only I'd—anyway. He told me *for the sake of the baby* that he should take custody.

I was terrified, but what choice was there? There was no choice. People who say there was a choice have never been in such a position. He promised he'd let me see Marietta. He was lying, of course—she came back to me when he left her behind. She came back to me when he left her. But I didn't fight hard enough. I can't forgive myself for that. I didn't fight hard enough.

Ursa still comes to me at night sometimes, especially in brutal cold. So maybe she forgives me. Maybe she does.

I see her face in the ice, her boot tracks behind me in the mud. I found one of her mittens in my woodpile, twenty years removed from when she'd dropped it in the Inland Sea while we were fighting a sturgeon the size of our boat. She's around somewhere, if you ask me. I go out to Magnetic Rock every December. She's, I'm—well. I'm still here.

I tell ya, honey—to love or be loved by an Abernathy means learning how to lose hold.

PAPER LOONS

1 DEC.

Lena: We'll all lose everything if you're not careful, so listen close.

Write everything down,

take pictures,

make records;   witness.

Capture as much as you can in ink and color and sound.

Then bring it down here, to the World Below. This is how you save us. This is how we remember the World As It Was.

I used to know but I lost my way. You'll have to finish what I started. If you don't, it'll all be black and cold, Lena baby. No light, no water, no more growing living things.

I've gone down to be with the Women   Beneath.   To keep safe. Come find me when you can.

Close your eyes and see yourself between layers. Speak to me through the air, if you need to. I'll hear you, darling girl.

Make fluid millennia, memory.

Everything can be a doorway.

                       Everything can be a hole . . .

A COWARD

[excerpt, interview with Patrick Bailey]

Emaline Alfred Bailey: When did you know about Ma?

Patrick Bailey: Not for a while.

When you met?

No. Yes. I mean, not really. Not from her mouth. Folks gossiped at the bar, in passing on the line. Everybody heard about the trial. But I didn't hear it from her until I'd moved out to the island. I think she wanted to make sure about me.

So everybody knew. Why didn't she ever tell me? Why didn't you? If everybody knew?

Look, hon. You're—it never mattered to me. I knew the moment I met you, I'd lay myself down in front of a train. You're mine. How do I tell you something like that? I'm a coward. I'm sorry. I'm sorry. Maybe part of me didn't want you to know. We didn't think you were old enough. That kind of story, you're never old enough. Your mother kept saying, *When she's grown and ready.* She wasn't ready. Wasn't gonna be. I wanted to tell you, but it wasn't my place.

Fine. But I knew. I knew something was wrong with me.

Not with you. Never you. Not her either.

Sure.

I guess a part of me hoped you'd never find out. I know that's naive, unfair maybe. Mar was [clears throat] it's been a hard time for her. I had this image of our lives on the island and it took me a long time to realize it would never happen.

What about me?

Honest?

Honest.

Every time you disappear around a corner, my heart spins a little in my chest.

(cont.)

No, he kept going.

I don't know, maybe ten minutes. Five. I don't really remember.

No, I didn't. I didn't really say anything after *I guess we better get.*

Yeah, he did. I felt—um, I felt him drip down my thighs.

What do you think? Yes, it fucking hurt.

He said, *I'm not some faggot,* and started the motor. He said, *Don't go telling anybody I am.* Then he pulled his pants up.

Uh, yeah he left. Left me there.

Naked. I was naked.

No, I uh, I couldn't find my pants.

I don't know how long I stayed after. I don't remember a lot of the rest of that night.

It was pretty cold by then. March, April? It was dark.

· · · · · · · · · · · · · · · · · ·

106. See also: pp. TK.

Yeah, I remember lying in the boat. Shaking in the boat at the shore.

He didn't speak to me for a while after that. Didn't make eye contact, acted like I was invisible.

Um, I switched shifts, called in sick.

It was fucking confusing.

I don't—I don't know. Shame?

If I'm more ashamed that he'd fucked me like that or, um, that I'd liked it.

I mean, I came, didn't I? That's what that means, right?

Yes. All of it. I regret all of it. I wish I'd said no the first time. I wish I'd said no when he came up a few weeks later and asked again—*You wanna go fishing?* I should've said no. I tried.

He asked a couple times and I begged off.

No, I didn't want to.

Well, he kept asking. And he made some joke about how he was gonna tell everybody what he'd done.

It didn't feel like a joke.

Because of the way he is. He says shit like that but he's actually serious.

Yeah, I believed him. So I agreed. But I didn't want to.

You think I should've called the cops?

Which of them was I gonna tell? Which of them was gonna believe me? They're all his fucking uncles. What if I tell them and they do the same thing? What if they laugh? What if they tell everybody anyway—

My fault? No.

I mean, I guess so, yeah.

I didn't do anything to—

Yes. If you want to think about it like that, none of this would've happened if I'd said no. But I didn't and we went back to Ruin Lake, and Hugo had his mouth all the way down my dick when my dad caught us that second time.

He threw me out.

I went and stayed with Ms. Orleans for a while.

No, Hugo didn't really seem to care about much. Didn't care my brothers beat the shit out of me, either—but then again, neither did any of you. So none of us should be surprised about that, right?

I remember exactly what he told me. *Your dad better not say rat. I got an idea, and you're gonna help me. You're gonna go along, or I'mma tell every-body you fuck moose in rut.*

Third shift.

I don't know, maybe two, three nights a week.

I, uh. I was supposed to be, yes.

It was only supposed to be me. Hugo wasn't supposed to be there.[107]

. . . .

107. According to records from the Office of Personnel, Mesabi Mine Co., Ruin
Lake Branch, the only staff on supervisory duty the night of 20 June 1999 was one E.
Olsen.

IT WAS SHE WHO REMEMBERED EVERYTHING

me.

THE LAND-CLUMSY, THE ONE WHO DROWNED, THE ONE WHO STANK OF ALGAE

CAELAIS CO. WILDERNESS SERVICE, RUIN LAKE STATION | 48° 4′ 15″ NORTH & 90° 39′ 19″ WEST

The Solstice, 20 June 1999, fell on a night with a full moon and a clear, cold sky, the wind out of the west across the North Country. Hugo was swigging moonshine and prowling one of the Mine's twelve-foot aluminum boats through the channels around Ruin. Ellis sat in the prow, a walleye line drifting behind them. Hugo had been cut from the slew schedule for the rest of the week, and having been banished from the Windigo by Walter Black for at least the rest of the summer he had nowhere to go and nothing else better to do. Idle minds and idle hands, as they say.

"He must've been expecting her," says Ingrid. "Your ma swimming, hand over hand in a neat, naked backstroke. When you're a kid, everybody loves swimming like that. Something claustrophobic when you're older. Think too much about what could be coming up around you."

Even from across the lake, the moonlight would have been so bright they could see her. Eyes straight up, stars reflected in deep teal-green, but her ears would have been submerged, listening to the night moves of the fishes and the diving birds below her, the shifting and creaking of the sediment, the watery breathing of her lake. I imagine Hugo cutting the motor, putting his finger to his lips. They would have drifted toward her in silence. Ellis would have blushed when she kicked and he saw the crease between her legs, but Hugo would not have looked away. He would have paddled closer and closer until they were within reaching distance of my mother, still deaf to anything above the lake, oblivious. Then Hugo would have lunged and grabbed at her with one hand, shoving at her face with the other. Her eyes suddenly huge, orbs white and wider than the moon.

She would have gone under in a swirl, slipped out of his grasp and come up dead quiet, saw who it was that had dunked her, then begun to swim on her stomach, kicking hard toward the shore. I imagine Hugo laughing, and Ellis smiling, uneasy, hoping the joke was over. But she would be only halfway to land when Hugo would rev the engine again and motor the boat slowly behind her.

Ah hell, Hugo, Ellis would have said. *Knock it off.*

Though I never met him, men like Hugo are easy to imitate.

What? Afraid of a little pussy?

Ingrid says the scene later suggested that my mother reached the shore, started stumbling barefoot upward over the sharp shale and muddy hillside toward the ridge where the Abernathy property used to be. Hugo jumped out of the boat and landed with a splash in the lake behind her; his boot prints were clear in the mud the next morning. She must have turned at the sound and slipped, ripping a bloody seam open along her arm and her spine as she slid down the rocks back toward the water.

"A pair of other miners found her next day," says Ingrid.

I imagine my mother looking at him and him looking back, both of them already knowing what was in front of her, already knowing she might fight and fail to stop it from coming. Her hands muddied, she would have reached behind her for a rock, then sneered up at Hugo, pointing when his pants dropped around his ankles.

So it's true, she would have said. *Mr. Skinny Prick can't get it up.*

I imagine her voice rang against the rocks, the basin of the lake, but there was no one else to hear her, and it sank into the water and was swallowed.

"Ellis would've hesitated," Ingrid insists. "Had him as a child in my outdoor explorers class. Cried when he accidentally stepped on a butterfly."

He may have hesitated, but he did not stop it.[108]

She was alone in the morning, when two other Mesabi men found her,

. . . .

108. Ruin is all sludge and moldering remnants now. Perhaps it is because the Mine left the wreck it made when it was done; perhaps because Ellis Olsen stepped toward Hugo and not away from him. What power it would take to make a man that huge—seemingly gentle, seemingly kind—watch while my mother was pressed down into the wet, stained soil on the shore.

floating facedown in the rotting branches of an old red pine that had been toppled into the lake by the storm the year before.

"Can't say nothin' on record," they tell me at the Bear & Bird. "Don't tell nobody we told you this, or we might lose our pensions."

When they pulled their boat up beside her, they assumed she was dead, that she had been for some time. Weak sunlight shone over the lily-weeds and frog eggs clustered in her hair. They put on their elbow gloves and dragged her into their boat. Ruddy brown water seeped out of her skin and her bloating limbs, then pooled at the bottom, wetting their boots.

"Near unrecognizable, but I could still see it was the Abernathy girl," says the first. "I mean, sorry. Your ma."

He tells me he remembers looking down at the dampening leather on his foot in disgust, as if he'd stepped in something putrid.

"We was on the team that bulldozed her house," says the other. "And here she was, come back to haunt us."

They say they wondered if *she was the kind who might have walked into the water on purpose*, though they couldn't be certain.

"You women are prone to doin' foolish things," says one.

"Gettin' sad, drinkin' too much whiskey. Forgettin' difference between what's soft and solid," says the other.

They say they went as fast as their little boat would go and they argued, voices raised above the roar, about whether they should bring her to the local police or the Caelais Co. Wilderness Station. Whether they should bring her body to anyone at all. They both worried they might be suspected.

"We coulda just put 'er back," says one.

"But then we thought maybe by the roadside," says the other. "Someone kind'd find her soon."

"Had to get 'er outta the lake," says the first again. "Wouldn't look good for the company."

"She didn't have no family to miss 'er," they both agreed.

They were ashamed of themselves for their cowardice. They say they really would have left her there on the road.

"Not sure we're any better than the Mitchum kid for that."

But it was then that my mother sat upright in the boat, spitting and coughing up Ruin. Both men scrabbled backward so quickly they should have fallen out or capsized. The boat rocked hard and the motor bounced on its bolts and came unhinged. They say she stared at them with such a blackness that they thought, at least in that moment, *Your granddad was right to think she was the Devil.*

When she reached up to pluck the lily-weed flowers out of her hair, it came out in clumps while a reddish color drained from her eyes. She shivered like she had been caught in a great wind, and then she pointed behind them to the shore. Her mouth moved. The first man reached back with his shaking hands and shut off the motor.

"I says to her, 'You speak?'" still clearly terrified at the idea she was able.[109]

---

109. No one knows for certain if it was Hugo, or Ellis, both of them together or neither, who pushed my mother under Ruin afterward, although almost everyone I interviewed, the Mesabi men included, had the same hunch. Regardless, that night the water made acquaintance with her lungs and stayed there, even after everyone thought she had spit it all back out.

THERE WAS A TRIAL[110]

[excerpts, official transcript, *Caelais Co. Case #1999CF0328:
State v. Mitchum*]

ATTY SIGARD SORENSEN: You are a member of the Mesabi Miners' local #386, is that correct, Mr. Mitchum?

HUGO MITCHUM: They put me on a slew gate quality assurance crew on third shift. Big fancy engineer position means we gotta make sure nothin' fucks up through the dark hours. Pay's not enough for anything except vice, but there ain't no other jobs up here, so I do it. Gig's all right—I don't mind the late hours, I make some friends. I feel a little queasy 'cause every day I drive in I gotta pass through an angry bunch with signs about sickly loons, poisoned infants, toxic water quality, but like I said— there ain't no other jobs up here. Those protestors sure aren't gettin' paid.

SORENSEN: Protestors like Ms. Abernathy's family.

MITCHUM: Yessir. The women anyway. Not sure I've ever seen a Mr. Abernathy.

SORENSEN: Have you met Ms. Abernathy before?

MITCHUM: Three times, sir, you include right now at this trial.

. . . .

110. Mid-December, 1999. Six months after she came back to life in the miners' boat, six months after Ranger Ingrid Solberg-Black took my mother's statement at the tiny clinic in Beau Caelais while someone stitched hundreds of black threads into the bloody mess that was her skin. No one expected the trial to come out in Marietta's favor, and it didn't. An excerpt I obtained from the county clerk's office seems to indicate even the prosecutor, Sigard Sorensen, Esq., did not believe her.

SORENSEN: Go on and elaborate, son.

MITCHUM: The first time was at the Windigo. Took me about twenty-five minutes to fall head over heels with everything about her, start dreamin' how she'd look in a white gown. I'm a romantic roughneck, always have been. Anyway. She takes me back to that weird little one-room cabin she keeps on that property behind the mine and has her way with me, me thinkin' I'm the luckiest goddamn guy, but the next morning, even before sun comes up, she wakes me up and tells me I got to be going. I try to charm her a little, offer to make her some breakfast, but she's not havin' it. She tells me she hates the Mine, has hated the Mine her whole life and before it, inherited the hatred from her ma and all the women her blood comes from. She says I'm cute but she can't do it, that she'll have bad juju forever because she slept with me anyway, and she doesn't want to earn more than she can pass along. So I leave.[111]

SORENSEN: Would you say you were respectful of her wishes at that time?

MITCHUM: Yessir. Ma taught me never lay a hand on a woman.

SORENSEN: Can you ascertain any reason she might have had to reject you other than your involvement with the Mine?

MITCHUM: Well, I've seen her around there a bunch, sir. Drinkin' and smokin'. I doubt I'm the first miner she met there. Maybe she felt shameful about it.

. . . .

111. I have found absolutely no evidence, nor corroboration from anyone in Beau Caelais, that my mother ever so much as winked at Hugo Mitchum, not to mention *had her way with him* and then threw him out of her bed like some kind of sixteen-year-old succubus.

SORENSEN: We won't speculate about that now, but thank you, Mr. Mitchum. And the second time you met Ms. Abernathy?

MITCHUM: About a week later, out on Ruin, sir. One night I'm out on a survey boat with Ellis Olsen, fishing off the side, when I see Ms. Abernathy floating like a dead frog on Ruin. I pull her up, both of us thinkin' she's a corpse that's gonna haunt us for the rest of our days. Turns out she ain't dead. Turns out she's alive and well, but she's a little drunk. Slurring and so forth. We took her back to shore in the boat, but she couldn't stand up on her own, couldn't walk. It was a little awkward.

SORENSEN: Why is that, Mr. Mitchum?

MITCHUM: Well, because she was naked, sir.

SORENSEN: So Ms. Abernathy was unconscious and without clothing when you found her, seemingly drowned in the lake, and when you managed to revive her, you realized she was intoxicated.

MITCHUM: Yessir.

SORENSEN: Were you involved at all with Ms. Abernathy on this same day prior to finding her there in the lake?

MITCHUM: No sir.

SORENSEN: So you have no knowledge of how Ms. Abernathy came to be in that condition.

MITCHUM: No sir.

SORENSEN: Thank you, Mr. Mitchum. That will be all.[112]

. . . .

112. And this from the fucking prosecutor. Because my mother was a minor, the police report, any accompanying statements, and her testimony at the trial had all been sealed, much like the pre-trial confidential deposition with E.O.—Ellis Olsen. What little voice she had been afforded was also expunged the day of her eighteenth birthday. The clerk of the Caelais Co. Court told me this is *customary policy*, and *if [I] have a complaint [I] am required to file a request for court transcripts* [which no longer exist], *attach an affidavit* [written re my interest in facts I do not yet know], *and petition with the District Attorney's office for an official Demand for Discovery* [re evidence I am and only can be ignorant of]—none of which I know how to do. I've also no idea why the court and its file clerks happened to expunge my mother's evidentiary memories, but left behind the awful legal humiliation of Ellis Olsen, also a minor at the time. To my knowledge, my mother never spoke of the trial to anyone again. And what reason did she have to speak up afterward? Hardly anyone in Beau Caelais believed her enough to get justice. Grief and guilt from well-meaning bystanders? The judge, one Hon. Miles Ironsen, dismissed the charges after only two days of testimony, for what is declared *a lack of evidence* in the court record. Her petition to reclaim the deed to my grandmother's land from the State was rejected for the last time, too.

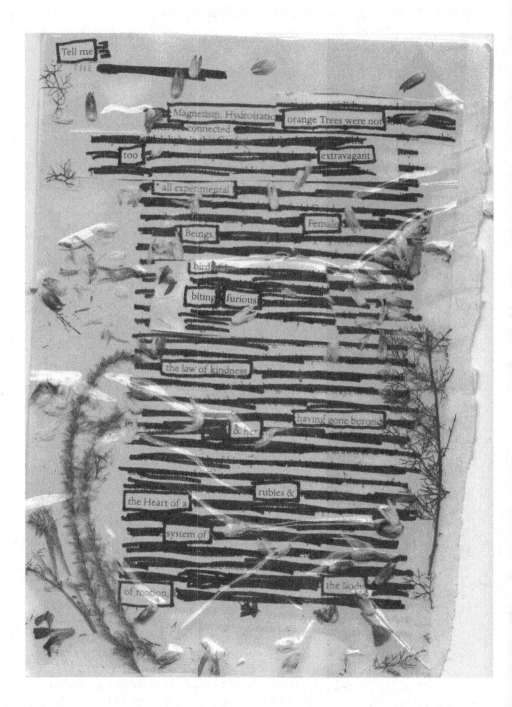

Tell me
THE

Magnetism. Hydrostatic   orange Trees were not
connected

too   extravagant

* all experimental

                        Female
Beings.

bird

biting furious

the law of kindness

                    having gone beyond

& her

                    rubies &
the Heart of a

system of

of motion.   the Body

THE ONE WHOSE HAIR WAS PERPETUALLY
TANGLED & SPECKLED WITH ASH

RUIN LAKE | 48° 3′ 6″ NORTH | 90° 30′ 18″ WEST

For seven days after the trial, no one saw Marietta Abernathy.

Bea says they waited up nights for her on the island, but my mother never came home.

Walter tells me she had stopped protesting in the parking lot at the Windigo.

Ellis Olsen and Hugo Mitchum went back to work, Hugo at least expecting to be greeted as a hero, but though the other miners had little love for my mother, none of them thought a young girl could deserve something so violent. Frank tells me he organized a fundraiser to pay my mother's legal bills, though he did not go so far as to give her the land back, or rally the company to rebuild her cabin.

"No one offered to pay for Hugo and Ellis," he says.

But then he tells me that he saw Hugo Mitchum and my mother near each other for the last time a week after the trial ended, though I could not confirm this with either for obvious reasons. The physical elements of the story are all from Frank Delacroix's account, collected at the Bear & Bird over shots of McGoggins. Their conversation is purely invented until the very end.

Frank says it was the first real snowfall in several years, the kind of heavy, wet blizzard that weighed down branches and showed off the black of bare trees in white quickly accumulating. He saw by her footprints that she had been walking along the side of the road toward Ruin, then finally spotted her, bullhorn in hand and three thin dogs trotting beside her—a black-and-brown shepherd, a spotted, yellow-eyed puppy, and a lanky, silver-colored thing that he thinks could have been a wolf. He also claims she carried a large black duffel bag, and that there was a pair of loons resting on her head, a crown of keeling, rippling black-and-white feathers.

"Real spooky," he says. "Like she had some kinda spell on 'em or somethin'. Folks always whispered about you Abernathy women, but I never believed until then."

Hugo had been driving in the other direction, likely going for a drink in the break room at the Mesabi office before his shift. Hugo being Hugo, he'd slowed his truck when he saw my mother, edged it to the wrong side of the road, and leaned across the seat to roll down the window.

He could have said, *Hey, there,* or,

How've you been? or

Need a ride someplace?

He could have said anything, really.

Coming from him, even something so innocent as *Hello* would have been enough to scare me off the road and into the trees, but my mother never scared so easily.

Hugo had slowed the truck further and rolled along backward beside her, looking from her to the Dogs and back again.

Where you headed, he could have asked, and

Fuck off, is how I bet she would have responded.

Frank tells me that he recognized Hugo Mitchum's truck and stopped immediately when he saw Marietta standing there next to it.

"I rolled my window down too, asked her if she was okay," he says.

He says her hair was wet, slicked smooth against her scalp as if she had been swimming and only just emerged. That she was wearing nothing but a worn black-and-white flannel that hung over her like a robe.

He does not say it, but I imagine the shirt concealing the beginnings of a bump that was me. He says she smiled at him and said *Everything's fine,* and then nothing else, instead humming something to the birds on her head, their large bloody-colored eyes reflecting the shadows of the trees and the snow falling all around them on the roadside. The Dogs were calm, he claims, except the pup, which was whining and pacing against my mother's knees with her ears pressed flat, as if there were an animal behind them or the smell of something unsettling nearby.

"I told Hugo to get," he says. "And I waited there in the road until he started his truck up. I was gonna offer to take her to my sister's place, get her some soup or a pop or somethin', but she and them dogs, those weird loons on her head—they was all gone when he pulled away, too. No footprints in the snow on the road, none into the trees."

I ask Frank if he knows what she had in the bag.

"All I can remember is it seemed kinda heavy," he says.

THIRTY THOUSAND ACRES

RUIN LAKE | 48° 3′ 6″ NORTH | 90° 30′ 18″ WEST

No one can definitively say they saw my mother near the mining office at Ruin that cold night, but the Fire started somehow and I like to imagine her, standing in front of the blaze and smiling. The mining office burned to the ground in minutes, and despite the blizzard, the flames spread to all the fallen trees that surrounded it. The fire ran the length of the Blow Down's wreckage and just kept running; it would consume near 30,000 acres before the volunteer crews could contain it. Dying trees cracked and split and whined in the wind. The Abernathy land smoldered long into the winter, until nearly twenty feet of snow had fallen and finally smothered the heat. For that one small moment, when the Mesabi propane tank exploded and took Ellis Olsen's right eye with it, she was triumphant. Everything around her must have glowed.

WE ARE WATER-HEARTED, HONEY.

Marietta Abernathy

I AM DREAMING OF A GUN IN THE HANDS OF A
MAN, MOON-SIZED AND BLIND

―――――――

[excerpt, *The Collected Journals of Marietta Abernathy*]

28 November 2016

Mitchum caught me on my way out to the Inland Sea tonight, so I got Patrick's gun down from the star-loft.

Beau Caelais's too small. I see him time to time at the market, on the street, just out here walking around, being alive. Pisses me off, makes me feel like I'm drowning all over again, like there's water in my nose. Sometimes I glare. Sometimes I look down. Depends on the day. Still, though, he's never been out here. Never thought he'd come near intentionally, at least not again. But tonight, this fucker just

shows up on the shore

of   my house,
my island,

like this is his now, too.

The Hole was getting harder and harder to find as the Inland Sea started to freeze for the winter, and it was supposed to snow the next three nights.

Patrick and Lena had gone to the mainland for driftwood, so I had the island all to myself. I'd piled up a load to bring Below—a fluttering, furry mass of moths, some tanks of freshwater lotus and trout, a few species of climbing mosses. Way back when, Hugo Mitchum used to come to the collections and step on folks' boxes, *accidentally* knock their jars of water into the dirt. *Oops*, he'd say. *My bad.*

When he came up on me in the dark tonight, I was already in my diving gear with a birch sapling in my hands, branches humming and rippling on the wind, all fragile and yellow. I had no choice but to put it down, or who knows what he'd have done. My fins make it hard to run, and the dry suit is like a straitjacket out of water, so he knew I was caught.

He smiled at me.

"Abernathy," he said.

The sound of my name on his tongue ripped me backward in time. He was clearly drunk. In the moonlight I could tell he'd not aged well—his cheeks had hollowed from his missing teeth, and what little hair he had left was wispy and slicked to the sides of his head. He stepped closer, and the smell of booze on his breath brought that Ruin Solstice moon out in the sky

like it was sixteen years ago Sunday,
like he's the one who could open holes in the universe.

In a way, I suppose he can. Does.

"You're not welcome here," I said, loud as I could manage. "You know it, Mitchum. Get going."

"Ah, now," he said. "No way to treat a guest."

"I don't remember inviting you."

He turned to look out at the Inland Sea, at the path his motor had cut through the weak, wet ice.

"Maybe after you give me a drink," he said. Stepped toward me.

"I said go back the way you came." My silver Wolf-Sister rose and bared her teeth, and the Shepherd Who Watches sat at my thigh. My little Spotted One slunk backward into the dark, but I heard her low, sing.

"Rowed all this way." He stepped forward again. "Man's thirsty."

I had not been this close to him in a lifetime.

"What do you want, Mitchum," I said, trying to sound like my bear-mother.

"Thought I might introduce myself," he said.

At first I did not understand what he was implying, and I cocked my head, thought for a weird, almost hopeful moment he meant to apologize. But I was not the one he wanted to meet.

"Where's the girl," he said. "Saw her after school. Pretty little thing, looks just like her daddy. How old's she now? Sixteen?"

I put the birch down then.

My ears   rang my whole   body went   hot.

"Stay the fuck away from us," I said.
The Dogs growled all around me.
"Stay the fuck away from me," I yelled.
                              "Get the fuck   back.
                                              Fuck off. Fuck off.
                                              I'll fucking   kill
                                              you,   Hugo."
"You're such a cunt," he said, laughing.
Held out his arms and grabbed at his dick.
"Be my guest. Burn it all down again.   See how far you git."

I spent the rest of the night bringing things Below. Not safe up here any longer. But it started to snow, wet, heavy flakes that made a whitewashed, billowing sheet of the world. Everything blurred at the edges in bright static, even my hands and my teeth, our little house on the rocks above the lake. My skin and the fabric of my old flannel, my socks.

I must be dissolving.

The ice was tenuous, thin. The farther out I got, the more blurred the shore became with the sky. The windows of our back porch frosted over and disappeared; our little wooden dock evaporated; even the stark form of the birch trees and the old black pine faded. Shades of blue glowed through the ice below me: pale eggshell, pearly teal, pewter, cobalt. Winter had been warm this year, and I could feel the water beginning to ache for the sky, threatening to break through. My head pulsed. My legs and my arms were so heavy.

I have to sit down.

I leaned back and watched the snow falling. Closed my eyes

they snapped   open   at a sharp report of splitting:
                              a huge blond man hovering above me.

He'd followed Mitchum.

Follows him everywhere all the time, I guess, because Hugo Mitchum stole everything from Ellis Olsen, too.

His hand was gnarled, but he offered it to me anyway. Lifted me up to my feet and onto the ice. Stared at me with that moonstone of an eye burned into his head, and I knew he was watching the Solstice over and over on the back of his lid.

He bowed a little, and I took both his hands very slowly.

"You," he said. "Queen of dark birds."

He knelt down, but he was still almost level with me. He shifted his weight and the sheet rippled. I wore my swimming fins, the dry suit, but I knew I could not have carried him if we fell through. Could not have carried his drowning if I had to leave him, either.

"Ellis," I said to him. "It's fine. It's fine, go home now."

It wasn't fine, has not ever been   fine. What does that word
fine   even mean?

I pulled at his hands, pulled him up like a tree trunk, and gently pushed him toward the mainland.

"You can go home," I said.

He shook his head.

"We made moon bones of you," he said. "I am ash now, yours for the taking."

"Ellis, I'm sorry, I don't know what that means."

He pointed toward the mainland, back at me. At the mainland, at himself. At the mainland a third time, and then took one hand and pulled it across his throat.

"Queen of dark birds," he said. "We made moon bones of you."

"Ellis—"

"No," he said. "No more."

And then he offered something I was not expecting.

I gave him Patrick's gun. I went to bed. I dreamt I was Below again.

Have you ever dreamt of a gun   in the hands of a man, moon-sized   and blind, of where he would take it and what he would do with its weight when he got there?

I asked around.

I showed the Women   Beneath all the scars on my back, how speckled and bruised my spine still shines. I asked them if they knew where I could find   God

I have a bone to   pick

but the Blinded Wife told me

we become and we unbecome[113]

· · · · · · · · · · · · · · · · · ·

113. *"Gott wirt und Gott entwirt."* —Meister Eckhart

and then the One with a Necklace of Handprints said,   *Ask &*
bring weather of the killing kind

    it was the Loud One who stood up and hollered   *no no no no no*
cheeks as red as the murky iron leech of   Ruin, that west end near
the put-in   where the wild rice used to grow, where the cattails
still shed   where mint and bitterberry run amok   they
shook and shook, took dead trout by their (skeletal) fins and smashed them
against the rocks   smashed their tiny hands across an accordion made
of abalone until the ruckus riledall those Women   Beneath,   every
one of us going batshit,   awful, shrieking,   all of us showing
teeth and tongue, bits of scars coming undone, broken ribs and shins (re)
rising, blackened eyes newly blue   again

       wheeze   *run, honey*   *baloney holy*   *fuck-around-a-*
heart-hon   *bloody*

   I tried to calm us down but we   kept hollering
   kept hollering
   kept hollering

until the Quiet One started humming

     little voice like embers   *don't think twice, it's all right*

only sparks

    but somehow this human with lungs the size of my palms insisted
    hey slow, hey

and we   listened
hey, we're all right *don't think*   *twice*
holy, we're o kay   *now*   *holy, we're oh-kay now* *honeys,*
      don't think twice,

don't think twice
don't think twice, it's all right, you're all right

holy hum rum ruddy

hum hum honey
and it was enough to   bring us back   into our bodies.[114]

I dreamt of a child who led us in some   harmony
some   gospel song that made mend   of   bone
holy   she sang   *holy*   we sang   *holy*
what a voice what a voice   *hum run*   *bloody*
    oh baloney roly poly   *we're all so*
holy   *don't think twice*   *it's all right*
she went round and round and round until we'd all joined, and then she
took that big

breath

that

    all at once   that air through the roof   wind
in   in   in

and from the star-loft, the sky split wide. It had been years:
but my mother the bear appeared.

Ursa!   she asked me where I'd left my wings

    and it was only then I realized
    I had no idea.

. . . .

114. *The Body Keeps the Score*, Bessel Van Der Kolk, MD.

I woke up knee deep in the Inland Sea. Ice,   high
water lapping at the door.

EVIDENCE

The conflict between the will to deny horrible events and the will to proclaim them aloud is the central dialectic of psychological trauma ... When trust is lost, traumatized people feel that they belong more to the dead than to the living.

— Judith Herman, *Trauma and Recovery*, p. xx

I saw her turn the fine bones in her fingers to feathers with my own eyes. Your people are wicked. Somethin' wrong with y'all. The kids at school had a song for her. *Witch, bitch, pussy willow . . .*

—Rita Mae Mitchum, mother of Hugo

The math, the diagrams, the theoretical structures of her continuum and what lay on the other side—it all made general sense, but I still didn't believe her. It was the emotional motivation, I admit. Had that not been a layer, who knows how far she could have taken the idea? We distrust things we can't explain on impulse, but truth is more complex, subjective, than we care to admit.

—Dr. O. M. Noyz, co-chair, Relativistic Physics & Wormhole Mechanics, College of the North Country

You've heard of the ghost dogs she had, those loons she kept on her head?

—Frank Delacroix, retired Mesabi Mine Co. site chief, Caelais Co. Aquatic Patrol officer

Folks in the North Country love a myth. The Loon Woman is a perfect example. How she turned herself into a bird and lived in the lake; how she lived alone at the center of the earth with just demon dogs and fishes for company; that she could never die because she'd done it once, and decided of her heart to come back and guide the rest of us toward goodness. What enchanting, miraculous tales!

—Lisle Bergstrom, Caelais Co. executive, 1993–present

Afterward, the Insomnia of Ashes. It was hellish. And I don't mean that as hyperbole. I mean a nightmare come down.

—Walter Black, former bartender at the Windigo

Consistent human ability to move between layers of the continuum would be dependent on recognizing the exact tangential connection where and when one wants to travel, a very specific, difficult, highly theoretical calculation that changes instantaneously. No one has been able to identify or observe these boundaries in any repeatable, tangible way.

—Prof. E. L. Cox, co-chair, Relativistic Physics & Wormhole Mechanics, College of the North Country

Why is it that the myths we hear about women so often make them passive spirits, deviously sexual youth, or the martyred truth-tellers in morality tales? Why does the name *nymph* mean both innocent child-bride and a slut with insatiable appetite for cock? We trap ourselves between two poles, and disallow anything more complicated and honest. I refuse this. Give me sirens who sing—it's not their fault stupid, arrogant men follow unquestioning to their deaths. Give me banshees, who foretell terrible things by shrieking and wailing so loud we can no longer ignore it. Fuck you for disbelieving us. Fuck you, blaming us for the sound.

—VJ Rose, advocate and chief agitating officer, the Loud Cunt Collective

WEIGHT

CAELAIS CO. WILDERNESS SERVICE, RUIN LAKE
STATION | 48° 4' 15" NORTH & 90° 39' 19" WEST

(excerpts, interview, Deputy Ranger Ingrid Solberg-Black)

You wanna talk about ecology, trophic levels, and we gotta remember everything builds around itself. Every piece has a place, and every piece affects its place, such that one ripples into the other. I think her Abernathy impulse—that thing in y'all makes you want to fuck with authority, partriarchy—gave her a certain kind of irreverence for the way we were used to thinking. She had weird ideas about preservation, conservation, environmental management. They weren't magic, just unusual. Thing is, though, after what happened on Ruin, and what's happened since—I think sometimes, *Was she the key?*

Marietta was only sixteen. I didn't really feel safe leaving her alone, but what was I gonna do, lock her in a room somewhere? County tried that, and she left. She'd've found a way through the wall.

Now, it's been almost seventeen years. Land's not ever gonna be the same, but we should have a healthy canopy again. Birch grows fast. Pine and cedar are resilient species. Even just a season after the Blow Down we had some good patches of the heliophilous stuff. Still, everything except the crows and those two damn loons steers hell clear of Ruin.

You ask most folks in Caelais County to name the guilty parties for the Fire, the Insomnia of Ashes after, I promise you will get one answer with three different names—Hugo Mitchum, Ellis Olsen, and your mother. You ask Ellis Olsen and he'd hand you a knife, show you his neck, name every soul in a hundred square miles except Marietta. Seventeen years later, man still can't speak of anything but that night on Ruin Lake. *Queen of lily bones*, he calls her, I suppose on account of how he and Hugo left her for dead in the weeds. *Dark birds callin'*. Guilt scrambled his brain, along with that eye. He knows what he done, and I don't doubt he won't stop sayin' it out loud until someone holds him responsible.

As she was the reminder, Ellis is the one remembering. I imagine every night is that night to him. Every time he looks at his hands, every time he smells the wind off the water. You wanna talk about guilt. There were things we all heard. There were questions could've been asked. We let him take it all, and look what it's done. At least wolves have the decency to tell the weak among them when they'll be devoured.

Everybody in the precinct, the Wilderness office, the forest rangers, the Aquatic Patrol, they blame your mother for Mitchum's death. It was Ellis Olsen that did him.

I was on third shift, which suits me because it's quiet and dark and nothing much happens aside from the occasional drunk in a snowbank, a foundering moose. The moon goes to bed and I go with it. Anyway. It was close to dawn when I heard the shot. He had cinematic timing, location. Same place Hugo left Marietta, he left Hugo. I was out on the sled with my dogs, last loop around the dead zone, and I saw him slinking away. Hands shining with what I'd later realize was blood. He even smiled at me. First time I think he's done that since 1999.

A BALM FOR ALL THE BURNS & BRUISES

THE BEAR & BIRD | 48° 3′ 6″ NORTH | 90° 30′ 18″ WEST

[excerpts, interview with Beatrice Orleans]

When you were born, you were a balm for all the burns and bruises we'd acquired in the months that brought you to us.

It was a clear, crisp day and the ice was just starting to break. She called me on the shortwave, wailing and cursing, and I came running. What else was I gonna do for my girl? I loved her mama, loved *her* like a mama, and Ursa was long gone. Closest thing I'll ever have to a grandchild is you, sweet pea.

Three days, Marietta labored. Moaned, knelt on her palms and kneecaps and bellowed, huffed, swore, paced and peed and bled down her naked legs, joked about death and turning wine into vinegar, lolled in the hot, raspberry bath I drew while she begged you to stop bursting through her pelvis, ate nothing but shortbread dipped in cream, climbed out of that bath, puffed, paced some more, moaned some more, swore some more, tore herself open while screaming in a voice I have never heard before or since, and finally you slipped into my hands and stared up at us, very quiet and wide-eyed, as if you had been waiting patiently behind a door that we had just opened.[115]

. . . .

115. I was born blue, like all the Abernathy have been. I would learn and love to swim, though not in Ruin—it is a dead thing now, littered with bloated trout and the empty shells of turtles dissolved under the acidic winter ice. Nor are there any birds, except—it is rumored, of course—for two common loons. People say they are the ghosts of a pair that once nested on a tiny island of red pines at the very center of the lake , but where they came from before that is uncertain. My mother used to sing to them, though she never told me why. She did not tell me many things, and certainly never told me this. Still, I know it is true because the air around Ruin smells of charred birchbark when it rains.

I AM DREAMING OF THE ONE WHO BREATHES IN SO MUCH SHE HOVERS

[excerpts, *The Collected Journals of Marietta Abernathy*]

22 June 2016

We were having such a nice night. I was bringing things down through the Hole, and I got the impression she was interested, maybe ready to help. But I left her up Above. I wasn't ready. Or maybe she wasn't.

I'm Below, in this house that I've built, all glass and bleached wood and fresh North Country flowers that haven't grown Above in decades. The water is clear, the sky is clear, the birds know how to fly upright. Even all these Women   Beneath, these ghosts I've known now for years—in these dreams they are all beginning to sew themselves back together.

The One Whose Head Had Been Cracked Open Like a Melon—she found a scarf, and now she loves how she looks in a mirror.

the One Who Was Left Sprawled in the Ditch Down Highway 61, they got up. They said, *Fuck this.* They said, *I do not belong here.* They said, *No one gets to decide where I stay,* and they. got. up.

the Six-Year-Old Twins Who Were Stolen—these two sweet kids, they're wiser now, and they're finding their own way back. They're drawing maps and taking photos with Polaroid cameras and humming sonatas they write in tandem. They fight, they go quiet, they wander off into the woods every now and again, but still, every day, they're making their own way back.

the Blinded Wife, she held her arms open wide one day and said, *Hey, assholes, y'all know I can't see. Can somebody help me find the shitter?* She makes everyone howl and she smiles and it doesn't matter that her eyes aren't there, because neither is her husband and now she's got ears like a fucking fox in a snowfield.

the One with a Necklace of Handprints—well, the handprints are gone. She still talks about them, but the bruises have faded. She breathes and she breathes, in and   in and   in

        sometimes she breathes so much she floats   slightly
off the ground,
        sometimes she breathes in so much   she hovers.

IT WAS SHE WHO BURST PIPES,
BONES, FLOOD BARRIERS,
IT WAS SHE WHO MADE A WORLD BELOW

HOME | 48° 12′ 57″ NORTH & 90° 55′ 23″ WEST

21 December 2016

I woke very early the morning of the winter Solstice to the sound of water running.

A cloud roiled black above the Inland Sea, a sour smell on the wind, and when I got out of bed, the wood was wet beneath my feet. Even in the dark I could see a pool forming under a crack in the star-loft. I looked out the glass and saw it was raining. Too warm for December.

But the seep was not just from the storm. In the darkest corner of the cabin, my mother was slumped in the bathtub, water overflowing the basin and spilling across the floor.

"Ma," I said. "What are you doing?"

She looked up, and reached for the faucet as if she were going to turn it off. Instead she spun the handle and the water roared, streaming past my feet. The water poured down the stairs, and I heard breaking glass, the Sound of Things Escaping. Her Paper Moon Menagerie, or what was left of it. What I'd managed to make of it. The loon in the globe keened.

She looked up into the rafters.

"Ma?" I asked, alarmed.

Her clothes were soaked and I saw how skinny she was, her ribs and her breasts pressing her slip. The slip was oversized, something I'd once worn and paraded in front of an old dressing mirror, my attire an unintentional farce of her own unraveling image:

> gaudy coral lipstick smeared across our teeth
> slender necks draped in strings of cheap freshwater pearls

two pairs of dirty feet pressed into two pairs of ratty pleather pumps

As I watched her shiver in the tub, I realized how young she really was. "You look cold, Ma," I said. "Why don't you—"

"Did you swim here, darling?" she said. "It's not safe. You aren't supposed to be this far out alone."

Then she sank herself under. I moved over to the tub and watched as she blew bubbles, the fabric of the slip wafting through the water. She held one hand up, still submerged, and spread her fingers against the surface as if floating behind a window. Her eyes went soft.

She opened her mouth

s w a l l o w e d

I grabbed at her elbow and tried to pull her out, but the weight of her wet body was more than I could lift alone. I ran to wake Dad, but when we came back to the bathtub, she had disappeared. A paper loon and a few black-and-white speckled feathers littered the floor, the trunk she called the Paper Moon Menagerie beneath the open star-loft window.

That night was what my mother used to call *a shedding storm*.[116] I'd heard on the shortwave the blizzard was to worsen for at least three days before it would be over, and I pretended to snore in the star-loft so Dad would go back to sleep, knowing the whiskey and the wind would keep him dead to the world until morning. After he slept, I crept down the ladder and out onto the front porch with the letter. The letter was much like the first one I had found three weeks before: folded and crisp and cold; inked to look like loon feathers.

There's a Hole in the world only we can see. Do you

. . . .

116. A shedding storm meant that *when it ends, when we come out on the other side, we've left something of ourselves behind. We are no longer who we were.* All told, it would snow a near-record forty inches.

want to see the World Below? Do you want to meet the Women   Beneath?

Go to the shoreline behind Ruin and wait for the moon to shine its way through.

There's an extra pair of loon-feather fins, and a headlamp, beneath the floorboards of the porch. Dive in, and swim down. Swim down as hard as you can, for as long as you can, until you see the Hole.

Bring him along when you come, if you can find him. He deserves a rest. Maybe the World Below will be good for him. Maybe he'll be good for us. Don't be afraid of him, Lena. I'll be waiting.

    I wrapped myself in layers, packed the loon globe and the dry suit and the fins into a backpack, and set out on snowshoes across the Inland Sea toward Ruin. The Dogs followed me out onto the ice, and though I tried to call them back, the Wolf-Sister had already disappeared into the storm. Rain turned to sleet and then to snow again. Without a compass or a line of sight to the horizon, I had to wait for breaks in the cloud to track my own movement off the moon's, and it was slow going. The wind drove ice into my nose, my ears, my eyelids. I could see only inches in front of me. Finally, the smoke coming from his woodstove gave hint at Ellis Olsen's hut. The snow had already piled high around it, and when the wind spit in my direction, the lake reeked of eggshells, old pennies.

    The Wolf-Sister waited from a strange perch on his roof, the Shepherd Who Watches curled staring at the doorway with her nose tucked into the ruff of her tail. The Spotted One stayed back, moving slowly through the drift beside me. I reached for the door and the wind came up; it slammed so hard against the outer wall I heard the hinges crack.

    I am a fool, coming here unarmed.

Ellis looked up at me from a plain chair all elbows and jawbone and bright, shining teeth, so large his knees came up above the table beside him. He was naked but for his underwear, his size fifteen snow boots. The rifle that rested across his lap looked like kindling. The hut sagged inward; the only light came from the glow of the woodstove. He squinted with his left eye into the storm, and the skin across his cheek curdled.

"You, queen of dark birds," he said, and pointed his bad hand—two mangled fingers and a stub of thumb. The floorboards creaked and the Dogs yipped and yowled as he stood.

If he spoke again, I thought, the roof would collapse around him and take the sky and the stars and me along with it.

I should not have come here.

I glanced around the room for a weapon: a cast-iron pan, a bucket of coals, the butcher's knife hanging above the sink—but still he held the rifle. I wondered if I could outrun him. He seemed to know what I was thinking and stepped forward. The floorboard bowed under his weight.

"The dark birds came that night," he said. "Blew ash in my eyes."

The loon on my back crooned, and a sound like a woman wailing came from far across the water. It reeled and repeated, high and plaintive. The Dogs howled in answer. I stepped backward, but he stepped forward again. His hair curled in damaged wisps at his temples. He hacked, wheezed, and his chest heaved; he blew, and poured forth smoke.

"I am what's left of your fire," he said, coughing.

I inhaled and starting wheezing, too. I turned and ran toward fresh air, bent in the yard outside his hut, but the wind shifted and smelled of old fire. Every breath caught in my chest; I coughed so hard I gagged. There was a rustle behind me, the sharp cracking of small branches and rock. I listened, stiff-limbed, as it moved behind me, lingered, drifted away. Just as I was beginning to relax, the loons started wailing at each other again, and then there was a hand at my back.

I had not planned to hit Ellis Olsen across the forehead with a rock, but when I turned to see him standing over me, time shot us both backward through a wound reopened.

Call it inherited PTSD, or

a permanent flight response   at the shadows of men growing low.

I heard his skull crack, saw his good eye go wonky. He buckled, and went down moaning.

"I'm not her," I said, quiet at first, and then louder. "I am not my mother!"

Blood trickled into his blind white eye from a sharp, thin split along the orbital bone. He lay there, spread-eagle, wide-eyed, and mumbling, tonguing the sweet iron dribbling through his teeth. He moaned about my *dark birds*, my *lily bones*.

"I made moon bones of him," he muttered, and groaned again.

"What?" I shouted at him. "What do you want me to do?"

But I already knew.

I pulled him by the boots out onto the ice, and at the very center of Ruin, I dropped his weight. Wheezed. The Dogs followed me down the hill—excited, nervous and snapping at the smell of blood. I stripped off my own clothes to put on the dry suit, and the Spotted One would not quit licking the soft of my knee, as if the taste of my exposed skin was reassuring. She leaned into me and whined. Her sister the Shepherd paced in tight circles around us. Their silver Wolf-Sister growled and leapt at shadows, dove snout-first into the snow, ran headlong out onto the ice and spun, yipping and impatient to begin what she knew somehow was to be done.

The hole in the ice was harder to cut than I expected. How many times had I seen my mother do it? She was stronger than I was. Is stronger than I am. When it was the size and shape of a man, the moon, all gravity and sink, I looked at Ellis Olsen, bleeding into his teeth. I strapped the loon fins onto my feet, bent down and wrapped his hands in mine, and took one long breath in. *Wheeze, hum, honey.* Then I dove.

We fell and fell and fell. Through blues and greens and grays, shadows and angles. A cathedral, a cavern, a Hole in the universe opening. When we landed it was hard—the air in my lungs knocked out entirely.

I heard a crack of glass—the Loon escaping its globe, one last wild sound as it flew away—into the lake? Ellis groaned beside me. I looked up. Beneath the ice there was no water, and I knew then she'd taken the entirety of Ruin and the Inland Sea Below, through the Hole she'd left for me to follow. Above me was not the storm, but an old mirror reflecting things that happened long ago.

There was the Solstice moon,
the clear Pleiades. There
was the silent shift of piney heads, the ghost
exhale of whistling birch leaves in wind. The World As It Was rotated and rewound and projected its recordings in loops on the ceiling of the ice. And then I saw the thing she had been keeping from me:

the hunting wake   of   Hugo Mitchum's motorboat, drifting behind my mother. I watched her younger, muscled arms slice through the waves, her teenager's hips rock along their strong, untempered axis. I watched Hugo Mitchum's hand press her head beneath the surface, the swirl of panicked water as she disappeared upward through time. She burst backward into the air and began to swim toward the shore, her palms and kneecaps visible in the shallow water and then gone as she ran up the hill. Just as he did then, Hugo Mitchum guided his boat behind her, splashed ashore, followed her onto the mud. Young Ellis Olsen came into the frame, his face blond and broad and kind, unscarred.

Below, Ellis seemed unaware of the scene playing out on the ice-lake-ceiling. He even looked happy, perhaps some euphoric benefit of concussed delirium. He stood, the underwear sagging from his skinny hips, one side of his bony white ass hanging over the elastic band. I looked around us. There were muted blue-green granite boulders, slabs of ash-gray slate, sparkling yellow-pink quartz and striated gneiss, but no plants, no fish, no life. I looked up from where we had fallen.

The Dogs looked down at me, a blizzard raging above them. Ears perked, eyes questioning. I whistled. The Wolf-Sister was the first to jump in. Her sister the Shepherd barked at the whirling snow twice before leaping. The last to come forward was the Spotted One, owner of a careful, timid heart.

"C'mere little," I said, and she whined. Finally she leaned down and let go, tumbling into the warm, murky air of the World Below.

Beside us there was a black blankness in the middle of a void, invisible, absent. Nothingness beckoning. The Hole was tangible and intangible both; best I could name it, we were at the mouth. If I squinted and peered left of center, at the core there seemed to be a door. A chasm, the size and shape of a door. I hesitated, but Ellis did not. He started toward the Hole and then paused, turned to me. He took my hands in both of his huge palms and pressed them to his chest.

"Dark birds calling," he said.

Made by the meteors, she had said once
on a night like this night, when the Ursids had started to fall.
The ones come down from the Great Bear.
I had never seen a star plow a hole in the ground.
There was no sound. There was no moon anymore, Above or Below, no light.
Made by the meteors, I murmured to myself. *The ones come down from the Great Bear.*
It was harder and harder for me to remember which way was up or down.
How do I keep track?
She had told me to use my senses.
They'll show you the way.
I was still hesitant to believe.
But I didn't see them, I had said.
No, darling, she'd said
Did you?
No, darling, again.

So how do you know that it's true?[117]

We learn to tell time from the sky, she'd said. *Read the curves in the earth.*

When did it happen?

Ten thousand years ago, dear girl, she'd said. *Before you were even a flicker.*

The air was dry and cool, and suddenly I was very tired.

117. I will wrestle with this the rest of my life. How do I know when to trust my intuition or tangible observation, fact or dream? Are they separate? Do I have to choose?

The Inland Sea, Below, was surrounded by a dome of stars like I'd never seen before, a sky unobscured by pollution.

It was not Upside Down, but the lake was hypersaturated in color, flush with the smell of plants and minerals: clean, potable, sweet. The surf was wild. The air was warm, and a big yellow moon hung low over the water.

The cabin she had built Below was tiny, barely more than that one huge window and a door set into a slope that cut steep down toward the lake. I bent at the shore and looked out at all the things she had been bringing Below. Submerged, they were now fast, healthy, whole. A rainbow trout I thought I recognized swam into the shallows, but its bulging eyeballs were back in their place; its beating-heart tumor inside its rib cage. I saw eyes in the reeds. When the wind picked up, I heard the sound of Women   humming.

I breathed in.

HOME | 48° 12′ 57″ NORTH & 90° 55′ 23″ WEST

If Marietta Abernathy is Hecate embodied

the Witch of the Birches and the Boundary Islands,
the One Who Could Conjure Other Worlds of a Moon Telephone,
Who Could Speak to Peoples Submerged in the Inland Sea,
Immer, immergo, immersus,

        the One Who Went Under,
the One Who Could Breathe Below

        it seems possible that I might be capable of magic, too.

But really, at best I am maybe   a mess.

        Of memories I don't understand, and mythologies,

spiritual roots.
Part selkie, part Odin's crows, a Nereid nymph misplaced in wild rice,
   whistling birch.
I am the granddaughter of a Banshee   and a Moon Junkie;
the daughter of the Devil,   and a strong,
   sweethearted man who plays blues on an old resonator, who carries clean
   water across the Inland Sea from the North Country.

I am maybe a reminder of what heat can do when it's let undone, when it
   runs, but

maybe I am also of the Women   Beneath, those Who Live
   Between Layers,
the One Who Was Made When the Water Came Up,
the One We Found When the Water Went Down.

Selected Bibliography

Calvino, Italo. "The Distance of the Moon." *Cosmicomics.*

Camus, Albert. "Absurd Freedom." *The Myth of Sisyphus.*

Carson, Rachel. "The Birth of an Island" and "The Moving Tides." *The Sea Around Us.*

Caelais Co. Missing Persons File #00400728. Filed 1 March 2010. Closed 3 April 2010.

Chödrön, Pema. *When Things Fall Apart: Heart Advice for Difficult Times.*

D'Este, Sorita. *Hekate Liminal Rites: A Study of the Rituals, Magic and Symbols of the Torch-Bearing Triple Goddess of the Crossroads.*

Deer, Sarah. *The Beginning and End of Rape.*

Dickey, James. "Falling." *The Whole Motion: Collected Poems 1945–1992.*

Erdrich, Louise. "Fleur." *The Red Convertible: Collected Stories.*

Fetter Jr., C. W. *Applied Hydrogeology.* 4th edition.

Huntington, Cynthia. "The Fish-Wife." *The Fish-Wife.*

Huxley, Aldous. *Island.*

Kimmerer, Robin Wall. *Braiding Sweetgrass: Indigenous Wisdom, Scientific Knowledge, and the Teachings of Plants.*

Kincaid, Jamaica. "Figures in the Distance." *Annie John.*

King, Stephen. *The Green Mile.*

L'Engle, Madeleine. *A Wind in the Door.*

Márquez, Gabriel García. "Un Señor Muy Viejo Con Unas Alas Enormes."

Nelson, Antonya. "Female Trouble." *Epoch*, vol. 49, no. 1.

Robinson, Marilynn. *Housekeeping.*

Rukeyser, Muriel. *The Speed of Darkness.*

Shiva, Vandana. *Staying Alive: Women, Ecology, and Development.*

Sibley, David Allen. *The Sibley Guide to Birds.*

Spivak, Gayatri. "Can the Subaltern Speak?" *Marxism and the Interpretation of Culture.*

Steinbeck, John. "March 18." *The Log from the* Sea of Cortez.

Van der Kolk, Bessel. *The Body Keeps the Score.*

Woolf, Virginia. "I feel certain I am going mad again . . ." March 1941.

Yehuda, Rachel. "Post-Traumatic Stress Disorder." *The New England Journal of Medicine.*

A Soundtrack for the Excavation of Marietta Abernathy

"715 - CREEKS," Bon Iver, *22, A Million*

"Black-Crowned Night Heron," Andrew Bird, *Echolocations: River*

"Cheap Wine," Charlie Parr, *Live at Terrapin Station*

"Dissolve Me," alt-J, *An Awesome Wave*

"Dream in Blue," The Stray Birds, *The Stray Birds*

"God's Country," Ani DiFranco, *Live at Carnegie Hall 4.6.02*

"Hell or High Water," William Elliott Whitmore, *Animals in the Dark*

"Hengilas [The Seafarers]," **Jónsi,** *Go*

"It's Alright," Matt & Kim, *Lightning*

"Lonesome Dreams," Lord Huron, *Lonesome Dreams*

"Moonshiner," Bob Dylan, *Live at the Gaslight, 1962*

"Only Skin," Joanna Newsom, *Ys*

"Ramblin' on My Mind," Robert Johnson, *The Complete Recordings*

"Saint Valentine," Gregory Alan Isakov, *The Weatherman*

"Slim Slow Slider," Van Morrison, *Astral Weeks*

"Sometimes I Forget You've Gone," Dirty Three, *Toward the Low Sun*

"Virus," Björk, *Biophilia*

"Way Over Yonder in the Minor Key," Billy Bragg & Wilco, *Mermaid Avenue*

feat. "Come Emalene, in My Flying Machine," Marietta Abernathy, recording on TDK cassette

Acknowledgments

First, a land acknowledgment:

This book was partially written on—and some of its setting and scenes modeled after—the (un)ceded and stolen lands of the Anishinaabe, particularly Gichi-Onigaming, the Grand Portage Band of Lake Superior Chippewa. There are neither words nor actions deep enough to heal the violence that white settler colonialism has and continues to visit upon Indigenous peoples, the land, and the water. The North Country and the Inland Sea are in part mirrors of the Boundary Waters National Canoe Area Wilderness/ Voyageurs National Park, and Lake Superior. Both should be returned to the Anishinaabe: #landback. For those readers who may not be familiar with issues related to land, sovereignty, broken treaties, Indigenous jurisdiction, the impacts of copper mining, deforestation, and oil/gas exploitation, or the ongoing generational traumas related to Missing and Murdered Indigenous Women, Girls, Two Spirit folks, and others, please connect with organizations like Honor the Earth and Seeding Sovereignty. Ten percent of any monetary benefit I received for this book (and ten percent of any I receive for it in the future) will be given to them.

Second, to the survivors I have had the privilege and honor of knowing:

To the Ones Who Have Lived: I will not name you here in respect for the confidence and trust you gifted me when you shared your stories, but I promise I forget none of your names, none of your stories. I carry you with me. You are the strongest and bravest I know.

To the young folks at Rosedale, the Ones Who Really Stayed at Sunday House.

To the people doing the work to build the Beloved Community.

Third, I believe in the impact of community, in the powerful love of (found) family.

To Geetha Shankar Iyer, for your concise and compassionate knife, for the ferocity with which you love me and my work, for your magpie brain and your archivist heart. Thank you for the playful way you subvert and reclaim linguistics, violence. Thank you for the space in your tree-house home, for the mangoes and maracuyá and bird-watching and sloth-walking and chocolates and strong coffee and late-talking and gin that would help me finish this book. Also many thanks to Martijn for his good heart, and N for her hugs and curiosity and being alive, at all in this world, startlingly and beautifully so.

To Lindsay Tigue (LT), my dear, wise, poet sister. For being an apothecary of memory, a buttress, a garden witch, an adventurer-out-of-sorts who shows me what it means to learn the boundaries of my own heart by way of testing discomfort and by speaking up when it is most hard to breathe. A pressure gauge by which I can set my own compass—there is no one else I trust more intuitively when it comes to language.

To Lindsay D'Andrea (LD), thank you for reminding me to return again and again to what makes me echo and yearn. Inquisitive editor, lover of the breathing of trees. Deep and joyful, someone who is hungry for the most delicious labor, as if this word work thrums in your blood, you *una cuore di fico,* you whose laugh I can always hear on this side of the ocean coming to shore.

To my other MFA/English program–mates, whose individual habits, histories, struggles, and successes as humans inspire me to work harder and to consider the world with a more inquisitive eye; whose encouragement has allowed me to take risks. Friends, kind readers, and vanguard against embarrassing prose. Thanks, all, for writing about your passions, and for living similarly beyond the page:

- Logan Adams, for your hearty roux and your punky soul;
- Corrie Byrne, crafter of obits and sweet sarcasm;
- Xavier Cavazos, whose voice is impossible to miss;
- Sean Evans, for the hikes and the whiskey and the blues;
- Sarah Huffman, brilliant and gorgeous, magnanimous and brave;
- Claire Kruesel, my favorite UU artist wildflower bodhisattva;
- John Linstrom, gentle poet-gardener;
- Mateal Lovaas Ishihara, fiercely queer, femme unbinaried
- Lydia Melby, for your prickle and your peach plum pear, forever forever for Totoro;
- Andrew Payton, a wanderer and whale-hearted love;
- Erin Todey, traveler, witness, teacher, friend;
- Megan White, you for whom the whole world is a *wunderkammer*;
- Chris Wiewiora, so gracious and particular.

To Ms. Miller, Mrs. Sallee, and Mrs. Place, some of my first readers—bighearted gratitude for your early encouragement.

To Kevin A. González, whose enthusiastic support began long before the work was remotely deserving, and to whom I owe an unpayable debt and at least three good pours of rye. Despite what strangers may think of you and your sardonic internet persona, your warm humor and kind heart have carried this writer far beyond our time at your office in Helen C and Mother Fool's. Abrazos and so many, many thanks, KG.

To K. L. Cook, who gave me the very necessary space and encouragement to consider such an experimental project in the first place, and without whom this would not ever have existed at all.

To Benjamin Percy, whose growling voice prowls in the back of my head whenever I am tempted to use too many adjectives or remain dreamily in description that does nothing to advance the scene. I could go on but won't, out of your respect for brevity.

To Deb Marquart, whose grace, sharp wit, and independent spirit guide me as an artist, and as a woman, and as an artist who also happens to be a woman. Thank you for showing me the enormous and altogether hard-to-come-by benefits of showing up in the world exactly in the ways *I* wish.

To Rick Bass, a giant of environmental justice and prose, both. Thank you for your generous time, your sparkling, mischievous eye. Thank you for leading me (us) up and down a snowy mountain, and feeding me (us) elk burgers and rhubarb pie. Thank you for showing me how to be a writer and a human at the same time.

To Dean Bakopoulos, whose phone call one sleety, awful day in February invited me to join the program that would change my whole life; who once told me I wrote a *cinematic* opening scene and that being enormous praise for me, someone who feels like their brain is actually a constantly running wrinkly taped camcorder. Thank you for teaching by practicing your own craft and your own mistakes out loud and in front of everyone.

To the other teachers who have helped me wrestle these disparate elements of my imagination into written form with some intelligence and creative structure: Amy Bix, Brianna Burke, Michael Dahlstrom, Kathy Hicok, Mary Swander, David Zimmerman. All of them generous mentors.

To some of the writers whose magic has fed me: Madeleine L'Engle, Louise Erdrich, Marilynne Robinson, dg nanouk okpik, adrienne maree brown, Anthony Doerr, Tim O'Brien, Annie Proulx, Julia Whitty, Chanel Miller, Ocean Vuong, Gabriel García Márquez, Tracy K. Smith, Aimee Nezhukumatathil, Muriel Rukeyser, Kevin Brockmeier, Maggie Nelson, Carmen Maria Machado, bell hooks, Danez Smith, Octavia Butler, Italo Calvino, Arundhati Roy, Elizabeth Bradfield, Barry Lopez, Pema Chödrön, Ursula K. Le Guin, Adam Zagajewski, Patricia Smith, Lauren Groff, Helen Oyeyemi, Ilya Kaminsky, Ada Limón, Edwidge Danticat,

Carson McCullers, Karen Russell, Czesław Miłosz, Barbara Gowdy, Sharon Olds, Rachel Carson, and Ross Gay.

To Sylvia Earle, Her Deepness; and Ed Ricketts, Doc Himself.

To the editors, judges, and publishers who have taken a chance on my work: Nicola DeRobertis-Theye and Sally J. Johnson at *Ecotone* for making "The Memory of Bones" my first published piece of fiction. To Susannah Luthi and Niree Perian at *Connu* for taking "Interviews After the Salt Plague" and featuring it as one of the first pieces in their innovative journal. To *Redivider* for "All the Girls at Sunday House Get Lost." Most especially to Chris Baker, Brenda Miller, Lee Olsen, and judge Marjorie Sandor for selecting "Things We Found When the Water Went Down" for the 2013 Tobias Wolff Award for Fiction at *Bellingham Review*, which would eventually shapeshift and transform into the book that is this one.

To Casey Gonzalez, early sorceress of editorial wonder. To Alicia Kroell, for your incisive penknife and your kind read. To Julie Buntin and Leigh Newman. To Andy Hunter, for carrying this project forward year after year.

To E Spray, the One Whose Sharp and Inquisitive Brain is Matched Only by Her Unwavering and Unabashed Affection. For the young moments we spent walking to school under umbrellas or at UU overnights; for the anchor to self and other you offered while we built roots and grew; for the gracious and gorgeous permission you keep manifesting to begin again, over and over.

To K Marie, my durio, friend of my mind, the One Who Laughs and Sings and Loves Like a Sunspot. Bear-hearted fierce protector of those who have rightfully earned it. You remind me of who I am, even though the visage has changed, the shape, the sound. We were born hours and feet away from each other, and it never has mattered how far and how long we spend apart.

To Cath, the Mountain Queen of Resilient Cake, for your bold and your bluster, for your soft and vulnerable self-reflective practice, for being a guide and an ever-present beam. So grateful we were happenstance matched, so glad I found a lifelong mirror. You inspire me to rise to many occasions, regardless of how I might be anxious or afraid—across continents, river crossings, train lines, tents, jungles, city sidewalks, hearts, memory.

To Amber, the One Who Transmutes Most Things into Complex Light. My hermanamiga. What would I know of the heart and the psyche and the soul, its intersecting Venn diagrams, if not for our years-long conversations? I can't summarize and I refuse to do so. You and I both know this can't quite be verbalized.

To Sandi, the One Who Teaches Me to Grow Things from the Ground, to risk it all on some wild scheme because fuck it, we'll figure it out, and to nurture small and miraculous things. For all the morning walks and the electric screwdriving, for the canning and the fiddle and the cat. For all the talking in between.

To Jaybird, the One Who Makes Easy Space for Everyone into the Early Night Hours, whose joyful and protective heart remind me to release habitual bruise, who reminds me of my worth. For all the bear hugs and the porch talks, and the delicious, unexpected cuisine, even if your Scoville index tolerance is far, far above that of my own.

To Shauna, my Queer Archivist, my Blueberry Allium Lyric collage, an exorciser and healer and most-critical-of-thinkers. For being found family and partner and Cat Dad and Van Enthusiast. For dance parties, road trips, fried eggs and kale, for insisting that we must all be Abolitionists, and for writing me love notes when I needed them most and didn't know how to ask.

To Maple, my Colorful and Exuberant, the One Who Adorns Themselves in Prisms and Whose Light Shines Out in Dirt and Kitsch Like Meow Wolf Come Alive, for gifting me a toolbox and filling it with utilitarian tools and gorgeous, campy accoutrements, and for knowing that both are so very necessary.

To Jenna, my Virgo Queen who holds power accountable in one hand and the most exquisite cocktail in the other, for your fierce and protective heart, your passion unmatched, your willingness to risk, for demanding we not be afraid of conflict when it is on behalf of a more just and humane world. For loving and believing in me just as I am, and for what you've reflected being revelatory.

To Lauren, the One Who Dreams in Lemon Trees, who is both more curious and far braver than almost everyone else I know, though you are quiet and sneaky about it. Who embodies authenticity even when you are not quite certain you know exactly who you are yet, and that being okay, because that just means you get to explore another lens, another mile, another story. For knowing your limits and naming them. For the photos, always, and for capturing the world as it is, in beauty and in starkness both.

To Virginia, the One We Call Grandma for being our fearless leader, the wisest and most kind, la Jamaica Violeta que Habla la Verdad al Fuego, but also the most gorgeous advocate and the One Who Heals by healing herself. For your incisive legal mind and your adventurous spirit, and for teaching me just about everything I know.

To Wilpina, my *jine-in-Majol*; the One Who Taught me *Iakwe in Bwebwenato. Kwoj pad ippa aolep iien.*

And to Aries, Suelyn, Ruby, Jordan, Monique, Rachel, Annie, Martha, Haya, Elise, Megan, Sara, Katz, Cody, Steph, Angie, CJ, Justine, Zöe, Len, Jerome, Baj, BB, Andrew, Adam, Asher, Greg, Marv, Anasia, and all the other anti-violence advocates I've been so lucky to learn from and love—evermore grateful for the strength of your voices, your hearts. This world Above is better because of you.

———————

To my Hamilton House family: Katie, Megs, Katherine, Andrew, Benja. It has been years since we spent such close time and still I never fail to feel familiar in your company. What a gift to be seen and heard and mirrored at such a formative moment. Thank you for the strong roots.

To Gillean, Megs, and KB, for being there at what always feels like the beginning, and for reminding me how much we've grown. For your selves as individuals, and as mothers; for the babies you are raising and how you are raising them.

To the Hamstars: Kent, the Theoretical Darkly Comedic Musician; Kurt, my misanthropic, taxonomic, ecological soul mate; Michael Pierce, you of the Blue Eyes and the High Mind and the Young Heart; Zach Parker, whose singer-storyteller energy made space for my amateur fiction so early; Ty, my dear, resilient, brilliant chef.

To Shakti: Daniella, Allie, Dubs, Ariel, Lea, Huntie, Steffry, Nicky, Val. How did we get so lucky, to find each other in that little store? How wild, in all the great wide universe, we got to spend so much time in a polytheist love kaleidoscope! I hope we get to spend a few hours in each of our next ten lifetimes giggling and burning Satya and eating at Himal Chuli and learning from sweet weirdos together.

To Joe Lynch and Lonna Nachtigal, for Onion Creek. For teaching me about basil jelly, buckwheat, garlic braiding, cider and kombucha brewing, ground cherries, hay-pitching, composting toilets, nettles, bluebells, morels, sunlight, drinking beers before/after hard labor, belly laughter, and love.

To Wilbur, for many years of brightness in the dark; to Pete, whose rambling mind is such a pleasure to match; to Coop, who taught me to spar with grace and spit; to Josh, who adores and advocates unabashedly; to Charlie Rae, Proginoskes embodied.

To my therapists, Brenda, Dana, Ann, and Jess, for keeping my brain and my body orbiting on a healthy axis.

To Leah Allert and all her horses, especially Domino, Willa, Leo, Big Ben, CC, Sox, Clipper, Chapeau, Pawnee, and Chance, and to Dover & Wrendog, for teaching me how to be quiet, still. Rest easy.

To my other dear ones—in Wisconsin, DC, Iowa, Minnesota, California, France, Ecuador, or the Marshall Islands, and elsewhere—for teaching me how to be a gracious, curious human.

———————

To Steve, for moosey days, kayaks, Granite River, and Irish sessions, and your continually generous eye. What a gift to have met you as a teacher and to have left with you as family, friend. To Clare, for tamales, fireweed, and loon calls. To both of you, for so much—but I'll start with blueberries, and Five Rocks.

To Morgan, who I raced across Loon and beat with my clumsy backstroke, and who taught me to reckon with the stories we tell each other about ourselves.

To Wilder, creator of Half Cat, my curious, artistic, thoughtful, daring, and kind-hearted nibling, for being the bravest and most open of humans. This world is yours and you need never bend toward what it says you must.

To Sarah, the One Who Names Us All in Ways Most Poetic and Precise.

Good goddess, what would I do without you? The humor, paradigms, and strengths with which you approach most things—cooking, tattoos, gender, road trips, pedagogy, grief, accountability, the wild wide expanse of the human heart—there is no one like you, my dear. Curious and critical, both of which we hold in highest regard. So grateful to have been pulled together, and so grateful to be able to keep you by choice.

To Josie, the One Who Sees Everything, the One Who Makes the Wisest and Goofiest of Jokes. Your generous heart gifts validation, affirmation, joy, and insight on the daily. J, you are the best chef, the most thoughtful and accepting of our family. Forever my sister from another mister and another mother.

To Spencer Adric, who was born and then some twenty-two years later introduced me to Charlie Parr, and therefore in both ways changed my whole life, who is wry and loves the North Woods about as much as I do.

To my parents, for always being supportive of my desire to tell stories, even when I was a toddler who scribbled nonsensical loops onto endless expensive computer-paper pages. To Mom, for being my first reader and best library advocate, and for your resilient and dauntless spirit. To Dad, for being my first listening ear, and the quiet calm that keeps us all grounded.

To my paternal grandparents, Robert Sterling Swanson and Margaret Pennington Swanson, for too many things to name. In short, for rainbow trout and red cedar.

To my great-grandfather Hugo, who I never met, but who I know was nothing like this one.

And finally, to Walker Henry Cardinal Pett. For seeing me, if only briefly. For supporting me through early drafts. For the opportunity to practice unlearning. For uncomfortable growth. For disappearing, and for leaving space so that I would build another World Below.

TEGAN NIA SWANSON is an advocate, educator, artist, gardener, and Unitarian Universalist Buddhist, most at home while in or near large bodies of water or walking under the canopies of many trees. *Things We Found When the Water Went Down* is her first novel.